STREET RAT

Fairytales with a Twist

JAYE PRATT
MELINDA TERRANOVA

First Edition.
Cover art by Emcat Designs
Formatting by Formatting and Design by Jaye.
Editing by Jenni Gauntt

To all the Disney fans, we hope you love our version of Aladdin.

This book does come with a content warning. While it's not overly dark, it does fall into dark romance and contains violent themes.

Street Rat, that's what they call me.

My reputation precedes me. There isn't anything I can't steal, acquire or covet.

I own the streets of Kingston Village, and everyone knows who I am. Except for the mystery girl Boo and I spend one lustrous night with.

I need to find her, but she isn't from around here. She may have been trying to fit in, but she didn't fool me.

When some rich prick tries to tempt me to find the underground club, The Lamp, I dismiss him until his phone rings, and her face flashes on the screen. He wants to throw cash at me to find something for him, except he forgets one thing *Never trust a thief.*

Finding The Lamp, lands me in a world I never wanted to be part of. I become the prized fighter for the mafia Don. The upside, his daughter is the girl I have been looking for.

Genie gives us an opportunity to be part of her world. Problem is she is engaged, and my best friend also has his eyes on her, and her bodyguard throws himself into the mix.

Lucky for me, sharing has never been an issue.

Street Rat is a why choose mafia standalone romance.

CHAPTER ONE

Street Rat

The downtown streets of Kingston Village; it's where the bottom of the barrel, the discarded, the people everyone have given up on live. Drug dealers, prostitutes, thieves, we're all there.

Street Rat, that's what they call me in these parts. I'm the best damn thief you will come across on this side of town, and everyone knows of me. If you need something, I can acquire it for you. Petty thief is the term the cops like to throw around. I prefer entrepreneur. Tomato, tomatoe if you ask me.

The main street is bustling with people this morning, every Saturday and Sunday, markets line the curbs, those from neighboring towns come to buy things for cheap, turning a blind eye to how the vendors acquired the goods.

Middle class working families, I don't mind them per say, even if they do think they're better than us. No, it's the rich, they're the ones I hate. My best friend, Boo, elbows me, and I notice the lady stepping out of the old run-down apartment complex in her designer suit and expensive handbag. She has little Jonas flanking her side with a sullen look on his face; this is the third time this year the poor kid has been taken into care. He glances up and notices us looking, and he smirks, wiggling his brows. He knows exactly who I am and the thought that crossed my mind. I didn't have plans for this today. Boo and I have our annual Halloween party to set up for, we had to come downtown to get our faces painted by Lady Trey, a drag queen that trades in goods and services. After the markets are packed up tonight, the streets will transform into the scene of someone's nightmare. Boo is going as a zombie, and me, my face looks like it's been ripped in half, Lady Trey is amazing at special effects make up.

Crossing the street, Boo beelines straight for the woman, and I come up behind her as she laughs at Boo—it's hard not to, he has a way with people. He could talk her out of her panties within minutes.

She hands him a business card, leaving herself wide open. She should have known better, bringing a purse worth five grand around here. Today she should have left it at home. Flashing your money here gets you robbed, or worse if it's after dark.

She doesn't see me coming, and I snatch the thing right from her shoulder, but it's no matter, her shrill scream will fall on deaf ears. No one around here gives a shit, what goes around comes around. If you didn't see anything, neither did I.

"Hey, you!" a man shouts.

Shit, market day might not have been the best day to take the damn purse, but Boo's sister, Siska, has been droning on about her birthday, and this would be a damn good gift. I'm known to give a good birthday present.

My feet slap hard against the pavement, taking a sharp left between two buildings into an alley, jumping a fence that leads to the back of a Chinese restaurant that's just a front for Ajax and his drug stash. I duck into the kitchen and wave to Mei; she shakes her head at me and mutters something in Chinese. Coming out the front entrance, I run into a soft body with an oomph, and I use my hands to steady her.

"Sorry," I mutter, looking into her big, round aquamarine eyes. My breath catches in my throat, she is the most exquisite girl I have ever seen, and that's an indication that she isn't from around here. I would remember someone that looks like her.

"Nice bag," she snorts, looking at the small bag tucked tight against my bulky shoulder.

"It goes with my face paint," I say, which entices the most beautiful sound I think I have ever heard in my life.

"Shit," she mutters under her breath as a sleek as fuck Ferrari rolls down the street.

Boo happens to pull up beside me in his beaten-up old Honda, it's a piece of shit and the duct tape holding the bumper on is the first telltale sign it's less than roadworthy. But beggars can't be choosers, and it beats walking.

"Need a ride?" he says with a cheesy grin.

"Need a getaway driver?" I ask the girl, a smirk curling my lips as she looks between Boos' car and the cherry red Ferrari Roma that's pulled up out the front of Miss Mayberries florist. I hope Boo doesn't see it, he will cream his fucking pants, and we won't be going anywhere.

"We won't kill you, pretty girl," Boo chuckles. "Corrupt you maybe, but never hurt you. We're real gentlemen."

That must convince her, or she's desperate to get away from the Ferrari owner, because she slides into the car and ducks her head down low. I watch as the douche climbs out of his red Ferrari, he definitely doesn't belong around here in his sharp suit and slicked back hair.

Ajax steps out of the Chinese shop and nods. "Want to do me a favor?" I ask him.

"It'll cost you, kid."

"Wouldn't expect anything less, go teach that guy a lesson in reasons not to cross town lines. People like him don't belong here."

He nods, and I walk around to jump into the passenger seat.

"Where to, boss?" Boo asks.

"Do you need us to take you anywhere?"

"I don't know, I need to kill a few hours," she says, playing with her hands. She really must be running from that guy, to get into a car with strangers who currently look like they would murder you and dump your body.

Boo looks back with a twinkle in his eyes. "Want to come chill at mine? A few of the crew will be there, and I can get my sister to take you wherever you need to be."

"You can trust his sister, the only girl with her head screwed on, on this side of town."

"Sure, why not," she says with a shrug of her shoulders.

Boo whoops and takes a sharp left, almost missing the turn off to his house. House is being generous. It's a run-down shack, but it's a home. His dad is a good man. He works long hours at the pub down the street, he also has a small drinking problem, but he doesn't beat his kids, and that's a lot more than I can say about most parents around here.

"My name..."

"We don't do names around here; everything is on a need-to-know basis. If you get into shit with the cops, we don't know you or your name. Same goes for you. The only time our names come up is if one of my boys needs an alibi."

"Got it," she says. "Then you can call me..."

She ponders it over for a minute.

"Princess," I say.

She makes a gagging sound, which spurs on Boo. "Princess it is, you can't give yourself your own nickname. I'm Boo, and that's Street Rat. Don't ask how someone got their nicknames, sometimes it's personal and sometimes it's not. You don't want to be on the wrong end of that question depending on who you ask. Mine isn't bad. My mum used to call me her Boo boo monkey, and it stuck more so after she died."

Boo pulls up out the front of our houses; we have been neighbors for as long as I can remember. My house is a little less run down, my mum likes to plant flowers and keep her garden maintained.

"Hey, Ma," I call as I climb out of the rust bucket of a car. She is elbows deep in the soil; she looks up at me and smiles.

"Hey, baby, looks like Lady Trey did amazing on your makeup."

"Face paint, Ma, I'm a man, I don't wear makeup."

"Hey, Lalah, the flowers are looking great."

"Hey, Boo boo, make sure you keep my boy out of trouble tonight."

"You not coming tonight?"

My mum shakes her head no, she will have a shift at the hospital. She should be sleeping right now but gardening is her happy place.

"No, I have to work as usual."

"All work and no play, I'm wounded that you can't make it as my date."

I elbow Boo in the ribs. "Stop hitting on my Mum."

Boo laughs, and my mum shakes her head. "You boys have fun and be nice to that girl, she looks new."

"Princess is brand new, I think we need to corrupt her a little," Boo says with a laugh.

We leave my mum to her gardening and head into Boo's house, finding Siska sitting at the table with her textbooks open.

"Hey, Sissy."

She glances up at me and smiles, it's no secret that she has a crush on me, but she is my best friend's sister, it will never happen.

"Sissy, this is Princess, we found her on the side of the road."

"Hi," Siska replies with a genuine smile. Siska doesn't belong here, she is a good girl with dreams, and both Boo and I have made sure that everyone around here doesn't touch her. She has a one-way ticket out of this hole. All she has to do is keep her grades up and get accepted into university. Boo and I have saved enough money to help her get a place to live when she leaves. We don't want her to ever look back at the shithole we call home. Hopefully she finds a boyfriend with goals, because if not he may end up with broken kneecaps.

"Hi, nice to meet you," Princess says, and Siska gives her the once over.

"I think we need to help you get ready for this party if you're going to stay. Those boys outside will eat a girl like you for breakfast."

Both the girls giggle, and Boo holds his hand over his heart. "Baby sis, boys like me would eat her for breakfast, lunch, and dinner."

Boo makes a V with his fingers and starts sticking his tongue out. I whack him on his stomach and shake my head. "Let's go out back and let the girls get ready."

I wink at Siska, she has been begging to party with us on the streets, but Kingston Village is no place for a good girl. Except this year I promised she could come, and I would convince Boo. I fucking forgot to run it by him, and I feel like shit. I wink at Siska, and I see the damn hearts in her eyes. I don't want to break her heart, and yet tonight, I have no choice, a guy like me isn't destined for greatness. I run these streets but her, she deserves a fucking kingdom and a man that will bow down at her feet.

"What do you mean the girls are getting ready? Siska isn't going anywhere," Boo growls.

"She is almost eighteen, she can hang with me," I say and then lean in close. "You can watch Princess."

He perks up a little and raises a brow at me, not believing I would let him have the fresh meat. He is right to question me. I plan to show Siska what kind of man I am tonight and try to let her down easy. "If anything happens to her," he says between clenched teeth.

"It's Siska, anyone would be stupid to touch her."

He nods at me, he knows I'm right. We have ran every man and boy away from her for years. No one would even blink in her direction and live to tell the tale.

"We will meet you girls outside."

Siska jumps from her chair and claps her hands before pulling Princess out of the kitchen and down the hallway.

I never feel bad for the way I live my life, but knowing what I have to do tonight has my gut curled up into a fucking ball.

Why did she have to set her sights on me? I'm gutter trash, and that's all I will ever be.

CHAPTER TWO

Princess

Princess, the nickname they gave me is laughable. If they only knew who I really was. Jazlyn Bianchi, daughter of Salvatore Bianchi, Boss or Don if you will of the fucking Bianchi mafia family. I'm a mafia princess, and I have literally put all of their lives at risk by coming here.

I know I shouldn't have run away from home. Every fucking soldier will be scouring the streets to drag me home. But what the fuck did they expect when my father announced my upcoming engagement to his consigliere, Armando Vitale, or Jaffa as I call him to piss him off. I wasn't asked or consulted about marrying a man almost ten years older than I am. I know you're wondering how he climbed the ranks so fast; he is a fucking weasel, that's how. My brother, Romeo, is the Underboss, so my father doesn't need me for anything other than a way to control me. He would counter with the fact it's to keep me safe. Which is laughable when he pairs me with a man who wouldn't hesitate to put a bullet in my head. Jaffa is all business and no pleasure. The stick wedged up his ass needs to be dislodged, and he may actually be almost a decent person.

"I don't have many costumes, but since they're calling you princess, I have an old ballgown and a fake crown. We can mess it up a bit and make it look like you have been attacked."

I look up at the girl they called Siska. My brows furrow as I wonder why they use her real name, but no one else does. It must be a power play, a way everyone knows not to mess with her. Maybe down here isn't so different to Willowdale, besides the difference in socioeconomics.

"What do you think?" she asks, snapping me out of my head.

"Huh? Sorry I was somewhere else."

She giggles. "It's fine. What do you think about this?"

She holds up a potato sack brown dress that she has added blood and rips into. I really hope this dress didn't mean something to her.

"It looks great, I hope it wasn't a special dress."

"Nah," she says, throwing it onto her single bed. "It was a cousin's wedding. I was forced to be a bridesmaid. We don't throw shit away here because you never know when it might come in handy, and now, it has a use."

Half an hour later, we are both dressed, and she looks stunning in a tight red dress that hugs her body, red wings on her back, and a love heart headband.

"I'm Cupid, what do you think?"

I laugh. "I'm not sure Cupid is supposed to look so hot."

She twirls in front of her mirror. "You think I look hot?"

"I do, whoever you're trying to impress is an idiot if they don't notice you."

Her eyes light up; it's always a boy, especially when you're seventeen. I know I was even though I was never allowed to date. I have more freedom now that I'm twenty and managed to convince my father to let me live on campus. I never cared all that much about where I went to college, but as long as I went and had some semblance of a normal life. I snort at myself, yeah so normal that your bodyguards follow you around all day. I don't mind per se, Gene, or Genie as everyone calls him, is hot as fuck. I like when he is on shift. I have a rotation of security, but the rest are dicks and would do anything to suck up my father's ass, it's all anyone ever does.

"I want to tell him how I feel tonight. I'm not a kid anymore, and I want him to see that."

"I hope you get what you're after, but don't put your self-worth in the hands of a man."

She nods, giving herself a once over, her fingers slightly lingering on the curves around her waist. If only she knew that real men love a woman's curves, high school boys are idiots and have no idea about real women.

Once she is done, she leads us back outside. The yard is full of monsters, zombies, and all kinds of things that go bump in the night.

I scan the yard for the only two faces that I know. Boo waves me over from beside a homemade fire pit, and the closer we get the more I can tell it's made from an old washing machine drum. Inventive, I give them that. The smile on Boo's face drops as we approach. Boo grabs his sister's arm and tries to pull her toward the house, but she reefs her arm from his grasp.

"What the fuck, Siska, where is the rest of your outfit? Go and get changed."

"No! I'm not a baby anymore."

She crosses her arms over her chest. Boo stares her down and shakes his head before stepping up onto an old milk crate.

"Listen up, fuckers! Anyone touches my sister, and I will put a bullet between your fucking eyes, got it?"

Everyone looks his way and yells got it, then Siska stomps her foot and huffs. "I hate you."

"Love you too, sis," he says with a smile that takes over his face and ruffles her hair. I glance up and his eyes run over me, and he snorts.

"I never thought I would see the day that, that dress looked good on anybody."

He takes a step closer, and he runs a finger down my cleavage. I know that I should slap his hand away, a man would lose his fingers for doing as much, but I'm not at home, I don't have to be Jazlyn Bianchi, mafia princess. I can be a normal girl and have fun and not worry about my every move and how it reflects on our family name.

When I look up, another set of eyes is watching me from beside the fire, and my entire body lights up. What if I just let go and had fun? Clearly, I have two I can choose from for the night.

Would it be so bad to have both?

My best friend Raj's voice fills my head, he is insufferable and the only person in the whole world who doesn't give a fuck about me or want to fuck me. Raj is bi, but he claims I'm not his type. He likes cougars. I snort, Raj is well just Raj and makes bank as a sugar baby to all the rich mafia housewives, but he will get his ass killed one day. He claims none of the husbands know shit, they think he is a personal stylist and his feminine ways have them believe he likes the dick, and he does. He tells me stories of some of the closeted mafia men he fucks. I live vicariously through him, but tonight is about me, and I have my sight set on two men.

Boo gets us drinks, in the form of cheap beer that tastes like piss, but I can't complain. After downing a few to calm my nerves, people start heading out to the main street where kids will be trick or treating and the guys help scare them. I feel like it's mildly inappropriate to scare the fuck of out small kids, but what do I know, my family kill people so I can't judge.

I bring the red cup to my lips and watch Street Rat from beneath my lashes. He hasn't moved from his spot for most of the night, he hasn't had to. People go to him, and I respect that. Siska sits next to him and fiddles with her dress; my heart sinks for her. He is who she has a crush on, and he is going to break her fucking heart. I know how loyalty works, I had my heart broken by my brother's best friend, Alexandro. I was so in love with him, hearts in my eyes and all, just like her.

"She has been in love with him forever," Boo says, sliding up behind me and wraps his arms around my waist.

"You know?" He nods against my shoulder.

"Yes, and so does he. We hoped she would grow out of it, but by the looks of it, she hasn't."

He pulls me back into him harder, and I stare at Street

Rat, his dark eyes locking with mine as he brings his cup to his mouth. "He wants you too."

Goosebumps line my arms at his words, and excitement thrills through my body. "Go break my baby sister's heart, so he doesn't have to."

I nod, but what the fuck am I doing? It should be girl power and us sticking together, but I wish Alex didn't have to be the one to sit me down and humiliate me by saying he didn't want me.

Downing the last of my liquid courage, I throw the red cup to the ground and step out of Boo's arms. Street Rat watches me as I walk toward him, his eyes locked hard on mine in a challenge.

I don't stop until I'm in front of him. I shut out the girl by his side and straddle his lap, this monstrosity of a dress bunching up around us. "So, I hear you're the big man around here."

His lips pull up into a smirk. "They call me Street Rat, Princess, whatever you need I can find it."

"Is that so?" I challenge, grinding myself against him.

His hand curves up and wraps around my neck, he slides it up slowly until he is holding my chin, and he assesses me. "That's really so," he breathes. "But first tell me what a girl like you would be looking for on this side of town?" Caught in his gaze, I bite down on my lip. "Are you looking for trouble? A bad boy to fuck your brains out, to show you how a real man fucks?"

I whimper as a body comes up behind me. "Tell us, Princess."

It's Boo at my back, he is crouched down behind me. "Does gutter trash turn you on?"

"I want to be free," I whisper.

"Do you trust me?" Street Rat asks against my lips.

"No," I whisper back.

"Good, never trust a thief," he says before his lips crush to mine.

In a blur of lips and hands, we end up inside, the room dark as we stumble through the bedroom door.

"Leave the light off," I whisper.

Hands touch me from everywhere, telling me this clearly isn't their first threesome.

CHAPTER THREE

Boo

Slipping up behind Princess, I slide the zipper to the dress down her back slowly as I press my lips to the nape of her neck. This isn't our first rodeo; we share bitches all of the time. Fuck, we share everything. He is the King of the streets, and I'm his right-hand man. Most men wouldn't want to be second in charge, but me, I don't mind it. All of the pressure would get to me, and I would be dead within a week.

"Look how well she responds to touch," I murmur, looking over her shoulder at the darkened form of Street Rat. My eyes have adjusted enough, but it's still fucking dark. I run my tongue up her neck, and she shivers as I suck her earlobe into my mouth.

I want to bite down hard, but I don't because I know she isn't from around here. I can smell the wealth on her. From the creamy coconut scent on her skin to the perfect manicure on her fingers and the bleached blonde hair that is not the bottle crap you buy from the drug store.

"Tell me, Princess," Street Rat says, "Have you ever had a cock in your mouth and one in your cunt?"

I shiver at his use of cunt. I'm sorry but it snuffs the fun out of fucking when he does it, and he knows it. Say pussy, vag, cum pocket, anything but cunt. I growl against her perfectly soft skin, and he laughs.

"No," she says with confidence. This girl doesn't seem to scare easily, but she should. If she only knew who we are. I guess our names don't precede us nor does our reputation. She is clueless and that sends a buzz right back down to little Boo. Nah, fuck that. It's a fucking weapon, and there is nothing little about it. I might not have been blessed with much in life, but someone was looking out, and I was blessed with a dick you could knock someone out with.

She steps out of her dress, and my hard cock grinds against her back, making her gasp. That's right, baby, feel how fucking hard I am for you.

Unclicking her bra with one hand is a talent few men can master, and she lets it drop to the floor with no hesitation. I'm almost jealous he gets to see those tits first; sue me, I'm a titty man.

"You have too many clothes on," she says, and while I don't think she is talking to me, she doesn't have to tell me twice. My gray sweats are quickly abandoned on the floor, and I step out of them.

Fuck this, I'm usually face first in pussy by now. I spin her around, so she is forced to look at me, and I smirk as I drop to my knees, hooking my fingers into her G-string and sliding it slowly down her legs, her perfect pussy just waiting for me. Without warning, I lean forward and run my tongue through her folds, opening her up. One taste, and my muffled moan echoes though the room.

I see him move from the corner of my eye as he drops behind us, and she sucks her ass in, pushing her pussy into my face. My laughter vibrates through her, causing her breath to hitch. Street Rat grabs her hips and pulls her back toward him. He is eating her ass, and by her reaction, she hasn't ever had a man that close to her tight little hole before.

"Oh fuck," she moans as we both hit her with pleasure from both angles. "Don't stop."

"Didn't fucking plan on it," he growls against her ass cheeks.

Spearing her with my tongue, her knees buckle, and her hands fall to my head. Her body spasms, and she screams, "Fuck!" followed by something in a different language that I won't even pretend to understand.

Before she has even come down from her high, I swoop her up into my arms and drop her down onto my bed. My cock is rock hard, and her breasts bouncing around have my balls so tight.

Staring down at the golden beauty while I palm my cock, her eyes go wide, and I smirk to myself. That's right, baby, this bitch is going to split you in half.

"Flip her," I tell Street Rat, and he nods. The fucker is all in for three-ways, but the clown doesn't like to fuck the girls. He will cork their mouth hole so my sister can't hear their screams.

He claims fucking means something to him. Laughable right? Fucking is fucking, and we are in our peak right now. Hot, ripped, and stamina for days. At least his Ma raised him right. The baddest motherfucker I know wants sex to mean something. It always means something; it means my balls are empty, and I won't rip someone's throat out tonight unless they come at me. And if that happens, I will be light on my damn feet.

He flips her over and makes his way to the head of the bed, moving in and kneeling in front of her. I move around to watch as she leans forward and takes his length, which is also impressive, just not Boo impressive. Her red lips wrap around his head, and I watch his head fall back and his eyes close. Fuck, that's hot. I move my hand up my cock in slow, measured strokes. Once he falls into a rhythm of fucking her mouth, his fingers twist into her hair; this is my boy.

I move to my bedside table and slide the drawer open, removing a foil packet. Street Rat is really fucking her face now, the drool and watery eyes make him hard. Kneeling down beside her, I reach out and use my thumb to wipe away the tears.

"Do you want him to stop?"

She shakes her head no, that's good enough for me. Pushing up, I rip the condom open with my teeth and climb onto the bed behind her, rolling the rubber down my length. I grit my teeth at how tight the fucker is.

Palming my cock, I run the tip up and down her pussy, making sure she is wet enough to take me.

"If you're a virgin, baby, pray to whatever god you believe in because this will hurt either fucking way."

I should be nice and take it slow, yet I won't because I don't know this girl, and come morning, she will run back to her side of town and always remember that time she crossed town lines and was fucked by the poor guys, who fuck liked animals.

"She just screamed around my dick, do it again," Street Rat demands.

I pull back and thrust again. "Fuck, you're so damn tight. Your pussy is strangling my cock."

Street Rat pulls back, and his cock pops from her lips. I momentarily pause because this isn't like him, normally he will empty his load in their hair. I snort at the thought; the prostitutes hate that shit.

"Don't fucking stop," Princess pouts. "Wreck me."

A growl comes from deep in Street Rat's chest, I balk at him. "Move."

"Could let a man cum first, fucker." I laugh, and he bumps my hip with his. Most men would have an issue with any naked part of another man touching them, not me or him. We're soulmates, and no, we are not in love. We get so much pussy we could drown in it, but are we open to a little touching between friends? Hell yes, or at least I am. I wouldn't have a prostate if I wasn't supposed to stick things in my ass. Makes sense if you think about it.

Last week that cocksucker dared me to wear a vibrating butt plug to a meeting. I came in my pants like a teenager and made a mess of my boxers. Never trust a thief, they fucking lie.

"Someone needs to start moving or I will fuck myself."

I pull my cock from her warm hole and throw the condom to the floor, and Street Rat flips her onto her back, moving his body between her legs, hooking one over his shoulder. His rapid-fire thrusts have her perfect tits bouncing again. If he won't come in her hair, I sure as fuck will. I take his spot from before, knelling above her head, and I cup my balls giving them a squeeze.

Stroking myself, my eyes move between her breasts, watching the way his abs flex, and his thick veiny cock gliding inside her warm pussy. She is so fucking wet.

"I can hear how wet you are. Fuck, that's hot."

"So hot," she moans, mimicking me. Street Rat isn't a talker; motherfucker normally gets his dick sucked and stalks out of the room like his ass is on fire.

"Squeeze your own nipples, baby, roll them between your fingers."

She does as I ask and moans, making my cock thicken in my hand. I'm so close I can feel a tingle deep in my sac.

"I'm going to cum," she whispers.

"Open your mouth," I warn before pure bliss hits me light a freight train and spurts of cum cover her lips. Her tongue moves, and she licks my seed from her lips. Her arms move, and she reaches around Street Rat and pulls him tight to her body.

"Oh fuck!!!!"

He must come at the same time as his body jerks. He pulls back and looks at me, his eyes wide. He is just now realizing what he has done. He looks from me down to her pussy before running his hand through her hair.

Never fear, Boo is here, I will fix this. I grab her legs and pull her down, so her ass is perched on the edge of the bed.

She clamps her knees shut, and I pry them open. "But he..."

I laugh. "Baby, we share everything, his cum doesn't scare me. Are you on birth control?"

She nods her head. "Good, but just to make sure, I'm going to clean you up really good."

And I do, I don't stop until her toes curl, and she is screaming out something in a different language again.

We just gave her a real Kingston Village welcome; it's how people like her get sucked into our world.

Street Rat hands me a blunt, and I smirk up at him, knowing my face is glistening with her pussy juice and his cum. He shakes his head at me, cups the back of my neck, and pulls me toward his face. His mouth smashes against mine, and he sucks my fucking tongue into his mouth.

I pull back. "If you want to taste her pussy, asshole, tongue fuck her."

Laughter vibrates from his chest as I light the blunt.

"Are you two together?" she asks meekly. We both turn to face her, seeing she has my sheet pulled over her body. I hand her the blunt, and she reluctantly takes it.

"Nah, babe, we just don't give a fuck," I say, sitting on the bed next to her.

"Well, it was hot," she says before toking and passing me back the J. Damn, who is this girl?

"Who are you, and where have you been all of my life?"

She laughs and lets the sheet fall down her chest, her perfect pink nipples making my limp dick stir to life.

"No names remember. And it's better if you don't know me."

"Why? Would your daddy disapprove of you being tag-teamed?" Street Rat sneers. Something is up his ass today.

"He would have you killed, but I just want to be Princess for the night, and you won't ever have to see me again."

"Fine," I say, pulling her up by the arms. "Let's go and scare the shit out of some kids."

We get dressed, and as I open my door, Siska is sitting with her back against the opposite wall as tears run down her face.

"Are you okay?" Street Rat asks my sister. She looks up at him, her mascara smeared down her face.

"You never would have picked me, would you?"

He shakes his head no. "I'm sorry, Sissy, I love you like a sister, I would die for you. I'm not good enough for you."

"Ain't that they truth," I chuckle. "Sorry, bro, but we are street trash."

He sits beside my sister, and her head falls to his shoulder. I wish there was an easier way he could have let her down, but honestly, heart break sucks. There is no easy way to let someone down. I'm glad her first heart break was him, because I almost feel bad for the next guy. We may be gutter trash, but no one hurts our family.

CHAPTER FOUR

Jaffa

"Armando!" Salvatore's deep baritone voice vibrates through the walls of his stately mansion.

He's lost his precious daughter in the slums of Kingston, where the dirty rodents and their seconds breed like the plague. The little bitch escaped my clutches and ran into the filthy streets, most probably lying dead somewhere by now. I despise her and her fucking stuck-up nose; the way she looks at me like I'm just her father's lap dog. Now that she's been promised to me, she'll soon learn what kind of lifestyle a mafia princess lives once she's been dethroned.

I stride into Salvatore's office and catch him throwing his expensive whiskey glass across the room. It shatters into a hundred pieces, and the malted whiskey stains the crisp white walls. "Sir." I stand to attention as always. My life is but to serve him, no matter the cost.

He turns and glares at me. The vein in the middle of his forehead pulses as his anger vibrates through him. "Find her," he grinds his teeth together, and I'm surprised they don't shatter from the force.

"Yes, sir." I nod, with no intention of hurrying to find that little bitch. I hope she gets what's coming to her, preferring to be amongst the riff-raff than spending time with me. Her indifference makes me impatient to own her and her perfect little cunt. I turn on my expensive leather Italian loafers and exit the room.

I make my way down the hallway and exit through to the kitchen where I find Raj sipping his espresso. This fuck stick is always around when he's not wanted. He irritates me as much as Jazlyn.

"Already misplaced your prized possession," he muses as he takes another sip of his coffee.

"Go fuck a housewife and let the real men deal with this mess your little bestie has put herself in." I storm past him and head to my car.

I grab out my phone and dial her bodyguard who is off duty today. "Genie, I need your help. Jazlyn is missing." I hang up on him as I know he'll be at our usual meeting point within minutes.

The family restaurant, Amici Trattoria, in the center of town is where we conduct business dealings and usually dispose of our enemies. It's one of many of Salvatore's money laundering businesses. I have to hand it to him, he's a smart man, always playing his cards to benefit himself and no one else. Only, I think that handing his precious daughter over to me will benefit me more than anyone else. That girl's pussy is my ticket to the top. Once I get a ring on her finger, she'll be mine to do as I please with. Her Papa won't give a fuck about her anymore. She will be my problem to deal with and the trophy I deserve.

I climb into my sleek red Ferrari Roma, ease out of the fifteen-foot wrought iron gates, and gun it to Amici Trattoria. I make it there in minutes and spot Genie leaning against his blacked-out Range Rover, sucking on a cigar. That man is built like a fucking brick wall. All solid muscle, covered in tattoos, with the street cred to match. I know he'd die for Jazlyn, and this is why I'm sending him in first. To clear the path for me to come in behind and be the knight in shining armor everyone expects me to be. It might make Salvatore forgive me for losing his daughter.

I park next to the Range Rover and climb out of my car. Genie eyes me as I walk toward him, unbothered by the news his little mafia princess is missing. "I need you to go to Kingston Village and find her," I bark at him.

He rakes his eyes up and down my Armani suit and settles his gaze on mine. "You fucking lost her?" He blows smoke into the air above him.

"Watch who you're talking to like that. You don't ask questions. You do as I say." I step toward him and then remember this fucker could kill me before I took my next breath.

He raises his eyebrows and sucks on his cigar again. "Where the fuck did you lose her?" He stands at full height, and we're eye to eye.

"Near some market stalls. She jumped out of the car and took off." I run my hand through my hair in frustration. I should have never taken her with me when I was tasked with finding that little thief, but I needed her Papa to see me making an effort of spending time with what soon would be mine.

"Fuck," Genie throws his cigar onto the ground and without another word, climbs into his Range Rover, roars the engine to life, and skids out of the parking lot like some fucking *Fast and the Furious* street racer.

I rub my temples as a headache threatens to pound my skull. I crack my neck before I climb back into my car and take off after Genie. I just hope to all that is fucking holy that she isn't dead. Salvatore will have my balls hanging from the rear vision mirror of his Rolls Royce on show for every fucker under him.

This part of town makes my skin crawl. It's infested with dirty scum that are more cunning than Salvatore himself. They weed out any morals in them young here, and they grow up to be devious criminals that outsmart most.

I pull up and park behind a fairly newish building, hoping no one touches my Ferrari, discard my jacket on my seat, and head into the decrepit streets full of market vendors and beggars. Desperate times call for desperate measures. The smells of spices and aromatic foods swirl under my nose, and I'm surprised by the pleasant smells as I wander further into the streets.

Market stallholders push their goods in my face and press them into my hands as I walk through the stalls. I haven't seen any signs of Genie, and I wonder if he has managed to get any leads yet. Surely someone would have seen a stunning, well-dressed Italian girl wandering around completely out of place.

"Sir, would you like to try our new cigars? Straight

from Cuba." An older lady with gray hair and deep-set wrinkles looks up at me.

I smile at her and am slightly saddened by the fact that she still needs to beg at this stage of her life. I reach into my pants pocket and pull out a wad of cash and place it into her hands. "Take a day off and enjoy some rest." I wrap her fingers around it.

Tears form in her old eyes as she places her other hand over mine. "Thank you, kind sir. May you be blessed with good fortune." She squeezes my hand before letting go and stepping back to stare at the large sum of money in her hands.

"Street Rat," she says, waving her hands. I whip my head to the side and squint my eyes. Surely that isn't him.

I carry forward, and I don't know if it's sheer fucking luck or that sweet old lady just granted me a wish, because about ten feet in front of me sits none other than the man they call Street Rat. I've been seeking him out for weeks now. He's always one step ahead of me, playing hide n seek with my men. But now I've set my sights on him, and I'll be damned if I let him get away.

"Hey!" I shout as I hurry my footsteps toward him.

He turns on the spot and looks as though he's about to slink out of my grasp once more when something registers on his features, and he crosses his arms across his chest and waits for me to approach.

A drag queen is perched on a stool, and this man who has a reputation to be the best at what he does sits there in a face full of makeup and a full blonde wig on his head.

"What do you want?" He regards me with caution. His dark glare matches mine, and I can see why he's the best. He looks every part the street thief his reputation suggests minus the drag get up, and he has that aloofness about him that makes it seem as though he could disappear right before your eyes.

"I have a job for you." I pull out my phone and see that Genie is calling, but right now my priorities are with getting intel on The Lamp for Salvatore at any cost, including his daughter.

"What makes you think I do jobs for people like you?" He looks me up and down, a look of distaste washing over his features. He stands from his stool and tells his friend that he will be right back before he grabs my arm, and his fingers dig in.

"You do jobs for anyone who pays the right amount." I point out the obvious. "Name your price."

"Name your job." He glances around to scope out if anyone is within earshot.

"Not here. Just know its not easy to find and could be dangerous." I narrow my eyes at him as he churns over my words.

"No," he says flatly.

"No? Are you fucking kidding me?" My anger simmers in my veins. This fucker is my last resort. If he doesn't do this, Salvatore will fucking retract my impending engagement to his sweet little bitch.

"I don't do favors for the likes of people like you and your organization." He uncrosses his arms and places his hands in his pocket, to grab his gun or knife or whatever else these thieves carry for protection.

I glare at him as my phone vibrates in my hand. I unlock the screen, and a video call pops up of Jazlyn's face.

She looks murderous as she glares into the phone. Genie's face replaces hers. "Good work, man. I'll be there in a few minutes." I switch off the phone and place it back in my pocket.

"I'll do it," he says flatly before he walks away from me and melts into the crowd.

I stare into the crowd and wonder how the fuck I'll find him again but know with slimy guys like him, he won't have any trouble getting in contact with me. I stride through the busy market back to my car to see Jazlyn and Genie standing too close for comfort. I eye them suspiciously as they talk quietly.

"You're unharmed, how nice for you. You can leave now Genie." I stare at him as he hesitates before striding away.

I step up into Jazlyn and press her into the sleek lines of the Ferrari. "Run away from me again and see what happens."

"Go to hell, Jaffa." She presses her hands against my muscled chest to try to push me off her.

"You reek of cheap sex." I wrinkle my nose to drive my point and reach down between her legs to cup her in my palms.

"Only you would know what cheap sex smells like." She squirms against me, and it excites me more than I care to admit.

"This is my ticket to the top, Principesa." I push my hand into her and watch her features morph into disgust.

"Not yet it isn't," she seethes and glares at me, not backing down.

"I love the way your heart beats faster the longer I touch

you. This will be the last time I chase after you into the pits of hell. Next time, you can stay here for all I care because I will have claimed you as mine, and I will do as I please with you. Get in the car so I can show your Papa that I found his precious little princess."

CHAPTER FIVE

Genie

That fucker lost her yesterday and is now in Salvatore's office cashing in on me finding her for him. He's such a useless fuck. I don't know what Salvatore sees in him to allow him to stay his consigliere. What I wouldn't do to end him and get him out of our lives, but I can't because for some unknown fucking reason, Salvatore has decided he's good enough for his daughter.

I stand guard outside her room. The press of my Glock against my back gives me peace of mind that if any fucker thought to come near her again, I'd put a bullet between their eyes. I don't know what happened last night, but when I found her with those two guys from the Kingston streets, I knew she would have been fairly safe. They weren't the worst of the worst among the criminals. Street Rat has a reputation for being the best of the best in theft, but I doubt he'd be stupid enough to murder a Don's daughter.

The way her eyes shone as she said her goodbyes made my instincts to kill kick in. Memories of the smell of sex on her caused my cock to stand to attention. I knew what had gone down through the night. Little Jazlyn wasn't so little anymore, and I needed to remember to control myself around her, especially when her Papa was around.

I'm not blind to the flirtations she throws at me, but I rarely bite back, because I'm trained and hired to protect her. Not dip my dick in her. It's hard not to notice how stunning she is. I see the way other men, including Salvatore's made men, look at her. She's the forbidden fruit that we all want, and the lucky son of a bitch that is about to get her doesn't fucking deserve her.

The door creaks open, and I turn my head to see what she needs. She's in nothing but a damn towel. It's wrapped around her just above her breasts. My eyes are drawn to the beads of water as they cling to her golden skin. My dick responds and presses against my suit pants as she stands there in all her salacious beauty.

She looks up at me with her doe eyes and blinks away the rivulets of water that cascade over her forehead from her dripping hair. She is breathtaking, and I bite the inside of my cheek to stop myself from touching her.

"Is Jaffa gone?" Her voice is laced with hatred as she says his name.

I turn to face her and block any view of her as she stands in the small space between the half-opened door and door frame. "He's downstairs with Salvatore getting recognition for me finding you." I stare down at her, and my gaze drifts over her pouty lips.

She swallows and takes in a deep breath. The attraction between us dances on the edge of taboo, ready to spill into the world of the unknown. The urge to reach out and touch her skin, to run my hand up her arm, over her shoulder, and wrap my fingers around her throat settles deep in me. I shift on my feet as our eyes lock on each other. An unspoken desire bounces between us, and one day soon, it's going to implode, and I'll be ready to claim her and show how she's supposed to be worshiped.

"Why do you put up with this shit?" She breaks the tension.

I step forward and crowd her space. "You know why." My voice lowers.

She reaches out and places her hand gently on my stomach. My abs tense under her touch and desire pools in my gut as she looks up at me through her long lashes. "It's not fair," she whispers.

"Life isn't fair, baby." I reach out and run my knuckles over her cheek as she closes her eyes and leans into my touch.

"Genie!" Jaffa's voice vibrates up the stairs.

I see Jaz flinch at his voice, and I reassure her with a wink that he hasn't seen our exchange. Even if he had, he wouldn't fucking dare tell a soul. He knows better than anyone how quickly I can make a man disappear, and I wouldn't hesitate for a second if he lay one aggressive hand on her.

"Go." She pushes at my chest, but her hand lingers there longer than intended.

"I'll only be downstairs. Text if you need me." I step away from her and head downstairs to see Jaffa waiting impatiently at the foot of the grand staircase.

He eyes me suspiciously, and I make a point of standing over him as I wait for his orders.

He steps back and glances up the stairs and then back at me. "Salvatore needs to discuss business." He flicks his gaze back up the stairs before storming toward Salvatore's office.

I follow behind him and enter the office where Salvatore seems to spend most of his time lately. He rarely visits his establishments anymore, and it makes me uneasy.

"Genie, you will need to stay with Jazlyn twenty-four hours a day. Do not leave her side. I am setting up the guest room down the hall from her room for you to sleep in. If she slips out of her room, I want you to tell me. If she goes to take a piss, I want you to tell me. She is not to leave your sight. Understand?" His eyebrows furrow, and the crease that forms between them seems to get deeper as the months drag on.

"Understood." A sly smirk graces my lips as I flick my gaze to Jaffa. I know he's jealous as all fuck right now. I know he thinks there's something going on between me and his betrothed. Well, now I'm going to make it my life mission to make his jealousy eat at him.

"You're dismissed." Salvatore nods at me before I step back out through the door with Jaffa hot on my heels. I come to an abrupt stop, and he manages to sidestep around me to face me.

"Keep your fucking hands off her. I see the way you two look at each other. She's mine, and I won't have my possession tarnished before the wedding night," he growls at me and reminds me of a fucking little puppy dog.

I step into him and push him back a step. "Call her your possession again and you'll disappear from this family. I don't care if you're Salvatore's favorite. Understood?" My nostrils flare in anger as his eyes regard me with a mix of fear and loathing.

"Watch yourself, Genie. You're not the only one here who has connections." He grins up at me as though his little threat scared me.

"Just know that when she's asleep, I'll be right there beside her." I barge past him and jog up the stairs to check out my new sleeping quarters.

The room has been transformed into a wonderland. I have all my security systems in place, including four screens that have live CCTV footage rolling around the clock. I step closer and study one of the screens; it's Jaz's bedroom. How interesting.

Whoever has set this up has already collected some of my belongings and placed them neatly in piles on the bed. Movement on one of the screens catches my eye, and I watch as Jaffa stalks up the stairs.

I move swiftly out of the room and head down the hall to intercept him at the top of the stairs. "Where do you think you're going? She said she didn't want any visitors." I cross my arms and glare at him.

He steps up onto the landing, leveling me with his angry stare. "Salvatore has ordered you to assist me in finding the elusive Lamp Fighting Club. I take it, you've heard of it before." He looks me up and down, and from that one glance, I know he thinks I'm beneath him. I also know he is full of shit, Salvatore owns the fucking club and I was the first to find it.

"What of it?" The Lamp is an elite underground fight club. Its exclusivity is what makes it so coveted. If you manage to find it, you don't just get to walk in you fight or supply a fighter on your behalf. Men don't leave the ring alive. It's fight until death in the last match. There is one reigning champion, and even I would hate to go up against him.

"Our mighty leader wants it, so we get it for him." He looks at me as though I'm stupid.

"And how do you suppose you'll do that?" I chuckle. This fool is delusional if he thinks they'll let him in by association.

"Don't worry your pretty little head about that. Just know I'll be in contact with you for your security knowhow." He pulls his phone out of his pocket and turns the screen toward me. "This is my ticket to getting higher on the family ladder. He agreed to help for a hefty sum, but it will be worth it."

I don't want to have to work with street scum but what choice do I have. I fucking hate that I know what his price will be. Jazlyn. I saw the way Street Rat looked at her. The same way I do, with lust, greed, and salacious desire.

"What do you need from me?" I was in. If for nothing other than to see this Rat and his Boo steal the one thing Jaffa wants the most. Jazlyn, his ticket to the top.

"To help me find Street Rat and Boo, so we can work out the finer details of their task." He places his phone back in his jacket pocket when his gaze focuses on something behind me.

"Did you say Street Rat and Boo?" Her voice trails over my skin, and I take in all her curves as she sashays toward us. She's dressed now, in a pair of low-slung loose jeans and a pink crop that shows off her tight stomach and delicious hips. Her damp hair cascades down her back and ends just above the curve of her ass.

"How do you know about them?" Jaffa narrows his eyes at her.

Her eyes slice to me in a moment of panic as she holds onto the railing to steady herself.

"They were hovering around the market stall when I found her." I quickly recover for her, but I know Jaffa isn't buying it.

He glances between us and then looks at his phone. "I'll trust you'll keep her away from scum like that." He pats me on the shoulder and retreats back down the stairs.

"Fuck. Do you think he knows?" She grabs my arm and demands my attention.

Her touch sends a turbulent desire straight to my cock. "I think your secret is safe, Princess." I wink at her and lead her back to her room. "I'm assigned to watch over you. I'm sleeping down the hall." I point to my new room. "So, please don't make my life difficult by sneaking out. If you want to go see these guys, I'll take you to ensure you're safe. Your future husband and your Papa don't need to know all your business."

She throws her arms around my neck and pulls me tightly into her. My hands rest on her waist, and before I can help myself, I'm wrapping my muscled arms around her tiny waist and pulling her tighter into me. The scent of her peach shampoo and coconut moisturizer swirls under my nose, and I breathe her in as her heart beats rapidly against me.

"Thank you," she whispers as she loosens her grip around my neck and leans back to look me in the eyes. She bites her lip as her thoughts go to exactly the same place as mine.

She feels so good in my arms and her curves fit like a glove against me. I lean in press my lips to her forehead, allowing my mouth to linger on her skin, to taste it and feel it against mine. "Come get me if you need anything." I emphasize *anything* because we both know I'd give the ends of the earth for this girl.

CHAPTER SIX

Jazlyn

Mixing my spoon around in my pasta, I sigh. Deep down I knew that night was a once off, yet I secretly hoped that I could see them again behind Jaffa's back. The thrill of pissing him off excites me.

My brother walks into the kitchen and looks over at Raj and I, and my damn heart does a nosedive as Alex walks in with him. Both dressed in expensive suits, their appearance is immaculate; my father wouldn't have it any other way.

"What's wrong Sorella minore, did someone hurt you, do I need to sort them out?"

By sort them out, he means hurt them in an unaliving way. My brother is as ruthless as my father, but he is one of my best friends.

"Nothing you would understand," Raj says, looking up from his phone. "Just boy trouble."

Both Romeo and Alex glare at Raj, and he smirks at them in return. "That's not wise, baby girl," Alex says.

"Don't baby girl me. Best friend's sister, remember?" I

snap, pointing at myself. I shouldn't take my mood out on him, and I know it. I'm wound up and need a fucking release, yet I refuse to screw Jaffa, that man will have to take it from me kicking and screaming. And Genie, well I flirt with him, but the guy is loyal to my family, and of course he won't risk my father's wrath.

"Jaz, don't be childish; you know as well as I do that our father has chosen Armando for you to marry. This is non-negotiable."

"What's non-negotiable?" my father asks, walking into the kitchen. Salvatore Bianchi is a powerful man, he owns every room that he walks into and that includes our family home.

"You declaring your undying love for me and me being Jaz's step-daddy," Raj jokes. My father's deep baritone laugh fills the room, and he claps Raj on the shoulder as he shakes his head.

"Kid, you couldn't handle me. Stick to your housewives."

Raj's mouth hangs open; he didn't realize Papa knew about his little adventures, but my father knows everything.

"Why do I have to marry Jaffa, Papa? He is deplorable, and I hate him."

My father grabs the coffee that Alex made and turns to face me and rubs his forehead with his fingers.

"I'm not going to explain it to you again, Jazlyn. It is happening."

"There is another option," Romeo says, and my father stops mid-sip of his coffee and glares at my brother. Even poor Alex freezes. Please don't say him, it's taken me a long time to be okay with Alex and I just being friends.

"Let's give her a chance to find someone by her twenty-first birthday."

My father opens his mouth, but Romeo continues to talk. "He must be from a family that could benefit us. You're always saying that we need to make connections for the future and how Jaz needs to step up more."

I look between my father and my brother, waiting for the yelling, but it never comes. Papa nods his head as he thinks, which is a good sign that he is going to say yes.

"Okay, if you can find someone that I will agree to then I will consider it."

Jumping from my chair, I wrap my arms around my father's neck. "Thank you, Papa. You won't be disappointed."

"We'll see. I will see you in a few hours."

With a nod, he leaves the kitchen along with Romeo and Alex. I haven't seen Jaffa today, but I can't wait to tell him the good news and watch his face when he realizes I won't have to marry him.

"I wouldn't get too excited yet," Raj says. "Have you seen the trolls some of the big players have for sons. Jaffa is a fucking dick, but the man is beautiful."

I scoff, I don't care how pretty his face is. I bet he has a small cock, and that's why he is such an asshole all the time. Raj turns his phone and eww. My face must portray my feelings because he laughs and jumps from his chair.

"See, I told you."

Genie walks in, and his presence alone could command a room just like my father's. The last few weeks he has been following me everywhere, and it's all Jaffa's fault that I have lack of freedom. I escaped from him once; I needed a break, and now I have eyes on me all of the time. I'm not complaining that those eyes belong to someone who makes me weak in the knees every time he walks into a room.

"Fuck, he is pretty in a grungy kind of way but don't even think about it. Your father would never approve it."

"I can hear you," Genie says. "And what wouldn't your father approve of?"

"Nothing," I say at the same time Raj opens his mouth, but before he can get a word out, I jump and slap my hand on his lips, and a muffled nose vibrates under my hand. Genie stares at us with narrowed eyes.

"Are you two ready to leave? If you want to eat before we meet up with your father, we have to get going."

Eating out with Raj is a mission, and Genie knows it. Who knows what fad diet he will be on this week, and he will need to grill the waitress on every aspect of what is in the food. Thank God my family own a lot of the restaurants in town.

After much deliberation, we settle on Vinnie's Pizzeria. My uncle Vinnie is the best, and while he isn't my real uncle, he was best friends with my grandfather growing up. Thankfully Raj is no longer on a carb free diet, so I'm not limited to what I can to eat. I'm Italian for fucks sake; every food place we can eat for free in this town has a menu full of carbs.

We walk through the door, and the smell of garlic fills the air. Uncle Vinnie smiles at me and rushes out from behind the counter. "Beautiful girl, look at you. Just as beautiful as your Madre, but don't tell your father I said that. He thinks you kids got his looks."

I laugh as he pulls me into his arms for a hug. All of my

uncles are huggers, but my father and Romeo didn't get that memo, they would shoot first and ask questions later if anyone touched them.

"Go find a booth, I will bring you one of everything, maybe two. That friend of yours is looking too skinny."

"You think I'm thin?" Raj asks.

"Boy, your cheekbones are sticking out, my nonna would be turning in her grave."

"Good to see you again, Vinny," Genie says, shaking my uncle's hand.

Raj and I leave them to talk while we find a booth, and luckily the night rush hasn't come in yet so we get our spot.

As much as I wish we could chill out here for a while, we have to eat quickly because my father expects us at the fights tonight. My father's secret business, The Lamp. I hate watching the main fights since the men that step into the ring leave it very hurt or dead. I love that Jaffa hasn't figured out how to find it yet. That is part of the condition of entry. You can't be invited; you have to find it. Genie plays a huge part in the fights. He organizes the date, time, and the fighters. Once you find The Lamp, you will get sent a time and code, and the fight will happen that day. My father thinks by making me attend that it will desensitize me to the violence. I think it's barbaric and a waste of time.

After forty-five minutes, Raj finishes eating, and Genie drives us to The Lamp. Genie pulls around to the parking garage, and we exit the Range Rover. I take a deep, shuddering breath in and blow it out slowly, putting myself into the persona Papa wants me to be. Here I am every part the Bianchi daughter. With my game face on, Raj and I walk side by side and Genie leads the way. No one here would be stupid enough to touch me, or even breathe in my direction. When we get to the back entrance of the warehouse, the door opens for us, and we step inside. The noise of punters screaming surrounds us at an almost deafening level. Genie puts a hand on my shoulder, and his touch burns my over sensitized skin and sends goosebumps down my arm.

"I have to go and work. Stay inside and find your father or brother and let them know you're here."

With one last searing look, he removes his hand as if he never felt a thing, and I'm left flustered.

"Girl, let's find your father before you leave a puddle on the floor. I wish you two would fuck and get it over with already."

"There will be no fucking."

Raj laughs and links our arms, pulling me into the open space. People move as I approach and make way for us. He leads us to a set of stairs manned by Jerico, who steps aside and lets us through without saying a word. We head upstairs to the VIP section where my father will be, over-looking everything down below.

The men at my father's table are all laughing and handing out money. The first fight of the night is over, and some poor fuck is laying in a pool of blood. Is he dead? Probably not. Manx, my father's top fighter, is normally the one who leaves his opponents with no pulse. He is the last fight of the night.

Looking down at the bar, I see that Camille is working tonight. Raj is already throwing money down onto the table to place his bets. His parents are filthy rich but never around, so they throw money at him, and he takes it and loves his lifestyle.

Camille waves at me to come down to the bar, so I nod at her and head back down the stairs. Papa might be strict, but he doesn't care if I drink; I'm almost twenty-one anyway.

Camille has my drink on the bar when I arrive, and yes, I'm a cliche girl and love a good fruit tingle.

"Any new gossip for me on the gang bang situation?" she asks, and I laugh.

"It wasn't a gang bang, and let's not advertise my sex life to my father's minions."

"Beer," a man demands as he walks up to the bar.

"Can I get a beer, please," I snap at him, and he turns to look at me with his beady little eyes. I haven't seen him around here before, but that is nothing new. There are a handful of new faces every week.

"I wasn't fucking talking to you," he snaps, standing to his full height.

"Well, I was talking to you, use your manners or..."

"Or what, little girl," he sneers, stepping into my space. "What will you do?"

He grabs my wrist and pulls me into his body as his other hand wraps around me and squeezes my ass. "Get the fuck off me."

I use my cool 'a Bianchi doesn't cause a scene, not unless it's 100 percent necessary' voice.

Camille screams and waves her hands around for either security or someone. Before I can do anything, the idiot is pulled off me and thrown to the ground, and a large body is over the top of him, reigning down blows to his face.

Within seconds, the men are pulled from the ground, and my father's men are standing behind them, pinning them to the spot as my father walks up with my brother flanking his side.

"What is going on here," my father demands, looking around at everyone.

"I couldn't leave you alone for five minutes without you getting yourself into trouble," Genie whispers into my ear, sending goosebumps down my arms.

"That bitch disrespected me and that guy attacked me. Wait until my boss hears about this."

My father nods his head, giving the silent signal. Romeo reaches into his jacket, and I close my eyes, knowing someone is about to die.

"Open and watch, you know how your father is," Genie whispers, and I open my eyes just as Romeo has the gun pointed on the newcomer who tried to help me.

"Would me putting a bullet between his eyes make you feel better?" my brother asks. Don't answer him if you want to live, it's a fucking trick question.

"Yes, and the bitch."

"Shame the bitch is my sister," Romeo says, moving the gun so swiftly the dumbass didn't even see his own death coming.

A shot rings out, and the poor guy slumps to the floor. No one says anything, and no one will. Who could possibly want to be in the path of the Bianchi wrath.

"And you," my father says to the other guy. "You think you can come into my club and cause a scene? We deal with matters privately."

"Papa, he was helping me."

I have to say something, I can't let the man die for protecting me. "I know and that is why his survival will be on him. Genie inform Manx that he has a new opponent tonight."

Romeo puts his gun away, and my father looks at me. "Next time, use your skills like you were taught."

"Yes, Papa."

He is right, I have three knives on me right now, and I could have used them, but then he would have lectured me on causing a scene. No matter what I do, I can't win. If only I was born with a cock my life would be so different. I wouldn't be a damsel in distress that needs protecting, I would be by his side.

My father and his men leave and head back upstairs since the fight in the background is still going on, and they need to have eyes on it. They stop for nothing and no one.

"You can't let him do this," I say, wrapping my hand around Genie's bicep. "It's a death trap, and you know it."

The newcomer scoffs at my words, but Genie pins him with a look. "If I were you, I would run. Manx is in the death match. Everyone that enters the ring with him dies."

"The thing about death is that you have to be scared of it, but I made peace with it a long time ago. Every day for me is borrowed time."

Genie shrugs. "Well, it's your funeral. If you win though, that man will give you whatever you want. He treats his top fighters well."

Genie takes the man to get ready for his fight, and I have to wonder how bad someone's life has to be that they would be okay with death so young. I, myself, have grown up around death. I first saw my father kill someone when I was ten, and I have been in therapy ever since. What kind of mafia family has their own therapist? Given, it's probably well known that if they talk, their life will end. Not that I'm stupid enough to give any details. We don't give out names. Huh...maybe I'm not so different from Street Rat and Boo after all.

CHAPTER SEVEN

Street Rat

The elusive Lamp wasn't that hard to find once I was on the right trail. Lady Trey is our town gossip, and her help led me to a few leads. When I kept hitting dead ends, I decided to find Princess. She seemed easier to find, and she was. That's how I ended up here. So, our princess is legitimately a mafia princess. Had I known that before I tried to pummel the asshole who was harassing her, I would have turned around and walked away. There are very few things in life that I won't do and fucking with the mafia is one of them. The reason why I won't fuck with them is the very reason I'm in this predicament now.

I text Boo and tell him to get his ass here now. I'm sure it's against their stupid rules to give away the location, but in the event of my death, someone should be here to drag my dead body home.

"What's your name?" the security asks as he takes me through a maze of rooms beyond the main floor.

"Str..."

He pushes a door open, and we step inside. The air is musty, and the space is barely lit, even when the light is flicked on.

"I know of you, but your street name doesn't mean shit here." I don't tell people my name, it's safer where I come from if no one knows who you are. "Save me the bullshit of no names. Salvatore will want to know who you are if you don't get slaughtered out there."

I snort. Seriously, he says that he knows who I am, and yet he has no fucking idea. No one beats me.

"Your ego will get you killed. Manx has killed more men here than you could imagine."

I shrug, he can suck my dick. The only people who know my real name are the people closest to me, my Ma, Boo, and Sissy. That's it.

"He can call me Street Rat like everyone else."

"Suit yourself," he says. "You probably won't live to see out the night anyway. I'm Genie by the way."

I shake my head. "So, how do you know Princess?"

He turns to face me and gestures for me to hold up my hands to strap them. If it's a fight to the death, does it really matter if my hands get busted up?

"You mean Jazlyn, I'm her security detail. I work for the Bianchi family."

Jazlyn, a nice name for a pretty girl.

"Can't say I see the appeal of working for the mafia, but whatever works for you. I wouldn't mind working alongside a fine piece of ass like Princess. Do you secretly fuck that tight pussy behind her father's back?"

His face drops, and his gaze turns feral as his hand moves to wrap around my throat. Rookie mistake, acting out of anger. He might claim my ego will get me killed, and maybe it will one day, but emotions will kill you faster.

He expected to have the upper hand, but in the blink of an eye, he is face first on the ground with my body leaning over his. He tries to buck back with his ass, but it's no use, he isn't going anywhere until I let him.

"Get the fuck off me," he seethes.

"Maybe I will, maybe I won't. I want to know what's in it for me when I win?"

"Whatever you want, Salvatore is a very generous man."

I lean in closer to his ear. "And what if I want his daughter?"

"Then I would say that name of yours better be beneficial to him. As a common street thief, he would kill you on the spot for even suggesting it."

I push myself up and into a standing position just as someone knocks on the door. Genie gets up and dusts down his black button-down shirt and pulls the door open. A beefy man nods at him and steps aside. A smiling Boo steps through the door.

"This place is bloody fantastic. Some poor fuck is going to die tonight," he sing-songs. "Connor here tells me the main fight is to death."

"Meet the main attraction," I say, and Boo looks around the room, but when he comes up short that it's just us and the security, he shakes his head no.

"Man, don't be fucking stupid. Think about your Ma."

It's not like Boo to be the reasonable one, it's why we are friends. He is always along for the ride no matter what it is.

"He doesn't have a choice," Genie mutters. "When the

Bianchi family say jump, you say how high, or a bullet will be lodged into your brain."

"Awe, man, what did you do?" Boo laughs.

"Funny story, Princess is a mafia princess, and I tried to defend her, long story short. I was either getting shot or fighting."

"Princess is here?" he asks as his eyes light up.

"Don't get any ideas," Genie adds.

"Too late," Boo jokes.

"Her father would never allow her to be seen with the likes of you two."

"Then lucky for you, because you know them, and if I win, you can help me convince him."

"I thought you said it was a good thing that our identities were hidden from her with our Halloween costumes, that it was a one and done," Boo asks, and I shrug. Maybe I fucking lied, I don't screw whores, and I don't screw strangers. But yet I wanted to fuck her, drag her down onto the depths of hell with us, and keep her there. I don't keep anyone around who isn't family.

"Maybe I liked the taste of her cunt and want seconds."

"Better not get yourself killed then," Boo says, clapping me on the shoulder. Genie looks at his watch.

"We better get you out there."

Boo and I follow behind Genie back out to the main area. He leads us away from the main fighting ring and takes us into a second room. Fuck me, a cage is set up smack bang in the middle of the room.

"Good luck, you will need it," Genie says, walking over to the man standing beside the ring, and he whispers into his ear. The man nods and looks back at me.

The roar of the crowd when the solid lump of muscle throws his fists in the air in the center of the cage is deafening. I watch his movements carefully, noting all his little ticks and nuances as he moves around the cage. From his sheer size, it looks like an unfair fight, but this dick is trained by professionals. I have the upper hand being trained on the streets, where we enjoy getting our hands bloodied.

"Fuck, dude, this guy looks like the business. Keep to his left, it looks like his weaker side." Boo slaps me on the back before I'm escorted into the cage.

I block out all the booing and screams for me to get slaughtered and concentrate on the fucker in front of me. He tries to intimidate me by beating his chest with his fists like a giant ape man. He just looks a moron, especially when I win this fight in a few minutes flat. I stand casually a few steps away from the exit and wait for the ref to throw the flag.

I can feel my steady heart rate as I concentrate on my breathing. I haven't had time to warm up, so I hope my muscles are ready to get used and abused. I bounce on the balls of my feet as I stare at my opponent and wait for my cue to pummel his face in.

"You're dead." He points at me, and a sadistic grin flashes across my face.

Bring it, fucker.

The ref drops the flag, and he charges straight for me like a fucking raging bull. I sidestep him in the last second, catching him unaware, and he smashes into the side of the cage, rattling the metal work. I descend on him from behind, and as much as a dick move it is, I pummel the back of his head in a three-punch combo.

He roars like a caged animal and turns his head to try find me when my fist connects with the side of his head, and I feel the crunch of my knuckles as they hit the perfect spot. I know he's done for before he even hits the cage floor. He lays still, his limbs at odd angles as his life bleeds into his brain from a burst artery. I've witnessed this many times on the streets, and it's always the cocky big guys that fall the hardest.

I've barely worked up a sweat as I stand back and watch the rush of officials storm the cage to save their prized fighter. I turn on the spot and find Boo where I left him. He winks at me and nods in approval.

The crowd is deafening as he lay face down on the floor, not a muscle twitching as everyone assesses him. The ref finally makes it through the throng of officials and holds my hand above my head, declaring me the winner. Boo finds his way inside and helps me to a seat where he shoves something up my nose.

The air around us shifts, and I look up as best I can through swollen eyes. The suits are all standing in front of me, their faces void of emotion.

"It looks like I underestimated you," Salvatore says with his daughter standing beside him, and my cock goes hard at the memories of her.

Boo clears his throat. "Most people do."

"What is your name, kid?" he asks, and I open my mouth, but Genie steps up beside Princess.

"His name is Alistair Barber, and his friend is Abel Andrews."

Salvatore squints down at me, and his mask drops for a split second. He turns to Genie. "Any relation to Alissa?" Genie nods.

"Her nephews, sir."

I wonder who this Alissa chick is and who she is to the mafia.

"Why are you here?" Salvatore booms, his gun whipped from behind his suit jacket and aimed right at me.

"With all due respect, we have no idea who you are, and fuck, we have no idea who we really are. Some crazy psychic told us to start with a Genie and a lamp," Boo says and snorts. "Could you imagine? Some digging, and here we are."

Boo has a gift to pull bullshit out of his ass, and lucky for me, his words seem to placate Salvatore, so he puts his weapon away and smiles.

"Welcome home, boys. As for your win, what is it that your heart desires?"

I look up and lock eyes with Jaz, but she rolls hers in response. "Unfortunately, I have promised my daughter that she can find herself a suitable man, or she is to marry my consigliere, but should you woo her, she might change her mind."

"I won't," Jaz says matter-of-factly. Oh, Princess, you have no idea. I'm a thief, I take what I want and that includes your fucking heart if I want it.

"Dinner, tomorrow night. Genie set that up. We have a lot to go over before your next fight."

"Yes, sir."

With no other words spoken, Salvatore leaves with his entourage, and Boo laughs.

Yeah, laugh it up, because I can tell that whatever name Genie just dropped will probably get us killed. I may have accepted my fate with death, working the streets does that to a person, but Boo, he loves life. He should walk away while he can.

CHAPTER EIGHT

Boo

It's normally me that gets us into predicaments that have loaded guns pointed at us. This Genie character takes us out through the back entrance and unlocks his Range Rover gesturing for us to get in.

"What the fuck have you gotten us into?" I ask, slamming the back passenger door closed.

"Fuck," Genie says, banging down on the steering wheel. "I will explain soon."

He peels out of the parking area and out onto the road. Street Rat is quiet, his poor face looks like it might explode from the swelling.

I press my nose to the glass, watching everything fly by. It might be dark, but I can make out how large everything is as we pass mansion after mansion. What the fuck has Street Rat gotten us into? We are too fucking poor to even be the help around these parts.

Genie pulls into a long driveway, and the house is dark, but the feeling of being watched washes over me. It's almost creepy. I'm not afraid of the dark per se. It's just jump scares really fuck with me, and my anxiety goes through the roof.

When they exit the car, I quickly follow behind, sliding up beside Street Rat. "I swear to God if the boogie man jumps out and tries anything, I will leave you for dead. There is dark and then there is this... Did you hear that?" I whisper.

"Stop being a damn baby, there is no boogie man here, and if there were, it would be us. We are what goes bump in the night."

Genie stomps up the steps and unlocks the door, reaching inside and flicking the lights on, thank God. He can tell me to stop being a baby all he likes, but my hatred for the dark stems from him. What sort of psychopath watches paranormal activity at nine years old and forces his best friend to watch with him? Street Rat, that's who. Now the paranoia has followed me, and his love of fucked up movies has followed him, and stupid me is right there with him, trying to prove how manly I am.

"Wow," I say, looking around the foyer, "is that a chandelier?"

"It is," Genie says, walking us past a set of stairs. We follow silently along a hallway until we enter the kitchen. One glance, and my mind is blown.

Genie goes to the fridge and slides a freezer drawer open and pulls out an ice pack. "As dope as this place is, what sort of bullshit have you dragged us into?"

Genie passes the ice pack to Street Rat, or should I say Alistair Barber. I snort thinking about it, and how the fuck he is going to be able to pass his gutter trash ass off as an Alistair.

"Me? Your boy got himself into a predicament. Salvatore would have killed him on the spot if he knew he was some low life from the other side of town. Especially if he knew that you both fucked his daughter."

"How the fuck do you know about that?" Street Rat asks.

"I'm Jazlyn's security, I know everything. Look, Alistair was my cousin, and Abel was a cousin by marriage. I'm trying to get to the bottom of who killed my mother. My search led to here, except they don't know that she was my mother. I had my whole identity changed after my family was slaughtered. Long story short, my mother and Salvatore were in love, but our families back then were at war, along with the Russians. They were forbidden to ever see each other; my mother was married off, and he married Jazlyn's mother."

"So, what you're saying is, we are taking the identity of some kids who died a long time ago, and that there is bad blood between the families and dinner tomorrow could be a trap to send us to an early grave?"

"Pretty much," he says with a shrug of his shoulder.

"Nope, fuck that. Street Rat, let's go."

I turn to him, and he doesn't move. "We can't, Boo, I put myself in that fight. Better he thinks I'm this Alistair person than knowing who I really am."

"He is right, Salvatore doesn't take lightly to people inserting themselves into his business and starting a fight. Even with good intentions, he has you on his radar. And after that fight, leaving now, he would hunt you down, and your families could become collateral damage."

"What the fuck! And you called me to drag me into this. What about my sister?"

"Calm down, I will figure something out, but for now, we stay. We can tell our families that we have a job out of town. That will buy us some time to have a game plan."

"You're going to need IDs, we will need to access money, and I have a heap that my family left in cash, but since you're alive, I can access it."

It dawns on me that this plan benefits him. "We might know someone."

"Good, I will send you the details. For now, you can use anything in the house, just don't destroy it. Same goes with the cars. Dinner tomorrow night, I suggest that you dress to impress. I'm sure you should be able to find something upstairs. Also try not to go back home, Salvatore will have you followed. If you need anything, I suggest you do it tonight."

"You're not staying?" Street Rat asks. I get why he is asking. Where we come from, you don't leave strangers in your house. Chances are when you get back there would be nothing left.

"I have to get back soon, I will see you again at dinner tomorrow night. I will send some groceries over in the morning to tie you over until we get your ID sorted." He takes a key off his keyring and hands it to Street Rat. "I suggest that you read up on my family a little before dinner. My uncle has a library here, and it has a family tree, and weirdly, a whole section with family journals and everything that you should need."

"Everything will be fine. I have bullshitted my way out

of many situations. Put your number in Street Rat's phone in case we need to get hold of you."

Street Rat hands him his phone, and once he is done, he hands it back. "Is there anything we need to know about Salvatore and his family?"

I'm glad he asked that question. "Nothing that you won't pick up fairly quickly. Salvatore is a businessman, his son follows in his footsteps, Jaz was supposed to marry Armando, but she has been given a chance to find her own husband. Though, I don't see Jaffa making that easy for her."

"Trust me when I say I will get her one way or another."

I look at Street Rat in surprise. His whole motto has always been to never fuck with the mafia, and now that he has had mafia pussy, he is going to throw all that away.

Genie goes on to explain a few other people who could be at dinner tomorrow night. Everything seems straightforward enough, now we just have to hope that we don't get killed.

I wait until he leaves, and then I corner Street Rat upstairs. He found a bedroom and is laying on the massive bed. I flop down beside him.

"So, this girl?" I ask.

"What about her?"

"You're willing to take on the mafia for her when you have only fucked her once?"

"So, what if I am? And it's too late to back out now, and she set me a challenge."

And there it is, it's got nothing to do with having feelings for her. He can steal anything, and he has it in his head he can make her fall for him when she said that she won't.

He must really be bored with his life to stoop as low as that. But fuck it, I'm on this now, and I say we steal the girl. Or at least her heart because fuck actually stealing a human. Okay I should rephrase that, actually stealing a girl because there was this one time where we kidnapped a guy, but he deserved it.

"Can we at least explore this place?"

"I'm going to sleep; you can do what you want."

I jump down onto the bed, lying flat on my back. "Man, should you be going to sleep? What if you have a concussion or some shit?"

"Then I die. Go find the information we need on this family so we can prep in the morning."

I sigh and push up from the bed, dragging my feet as I make my way out of the room. Finding this library of books wasn't hard, or the section on this Barber family. What sort of narcissists have a section just for their family? Your legacy is built through your actions, things you will tell your grandkids and they will tell theirs.

I make a stack of books to take downstairs, the ones with the family trees and the who is who. Hopefully we can retain as much information as we can, because neither of us is book smart. I can talk my way out of almost anything, I'm just not confident that applies to the mafia and their trigger fingers. I'm too pretty to die this young, I have so much more fucking to do and chaos to cause. It's not my time, and if I do get killed, I'm going to come back and haunt Street Rat for the rest of his miserable life. I can't be too mad at him, though. It's usually me that gets us into these kinds of situations, so it's nice to be on the other end for a change.

CHAPTER NINE

Genie

I pull up at the entrance to Salvatore's Pantheon Hotel, fighting the feeling to cringe. The glitz and glamor of this place makes me feel uncomfortable.

"Any chance that you will stay in the car?" I glance at Jaz as I exit and hope she listens to me. Who am I kidding, she isn't staying in the car. I stride around to the passenger side and push the valet aside as I open her car door and hold out a hand for her to take.

She looks at me like I've grown a second head and takes my hand anyway. "You know, I can walk by myself." She side-eyes me, but I know she loves the attention. "Isn't this taking your job a little too far?"

I lean into her ear to whisper. "Too far would be balls deep inside you." I hear her sharp intake of air as I lead her through the lobby doors and to the private dining room. I have never been this brazen with her, but what if this is my chance to spend a night with her? I know once I find out the truth about my family, I will have to leave or take my rightful place in my family. For a split second, I let myself think about taking Jaz as my own. Stupid fucking idea. Salvatore won't let me live when he finds out who I am.

The room full of men stand as she makes her entrance, and I see the way Street Rat, Boo, and Jaffa eye her with lust. The silence as she makes her way around the table and commands the attention of all the men is notable.

I follow her dutifully until she takes her place beside her Papa. He kisses her on the cheek, and once she sits, all the other men take their seats again. I move to my position beside her and throw a knowing look at Jaffa, who sits at the other end of the table where his place should always be.

Boo and Street Rat scrub up pretty well. I see they have made good use of the house already. They look like two respectable young men from the right side of the tracks. The suits they wear fit as though they were truly meant for them. I just hope to fuck they have done their homework and read up on both the families, because if this comes unstuck, I can bet their heads will be removed from their shoulders. Salvatore doesn't suffer fools or liars.

I nod in their direction, and they nod slyly in response. Always on guard in unfamiliar territory.

"Get my man a drink," Romeo calls to the waiter standing at the door. "You must be fucking thirsty looking after Jazlyn's needy ass all day," he chuckles.

There are things I want to do to her ass, I think to myself. "She's no trouble, really." I glance around the table and eye everyone as they chat amongst themselves.

"Alistair, I expect you are enjoying your new lifestyle?" Salvatore's voice carries across the room.

Street Rat glances up from the private conversation he

and Boo were having. "It's going to take some time to get used to. The luxuries are a nice change, but my heart will always remain back home."

"Not for me, I'm lapping this shit up. Give me all the glittery diamonds and shiny gold." Boo salutes with his tumbler and throws back his drink before asking the waiter to refill his drink.

"Boys. This is a lifestyle that one does not take for granted as any minute it can be ripped out from under you. Savor every damn minute while you can." Salvatore lifts his glass, and we all follow suit.

"To ruthless fuckers and the men that fear them," Boo chants and grins from ear to ear.

"So, Alistair, where did you learn to fight so ruthlessly?" Jaffa glares at Street Rat.

Street Rat sits up straighter, and his gaze narrows. "The streets. We fight to live. There are no rules like in the ring. If you don't learn to protect yourself, you're as good as dead." Street Rat's gaze slinks to Jazlyn, and their eyes lock for a heated moment.

Jaffa follows his gaze and watches intently as Jazlyn blushes, and I can see the jealousy roll off him in waves. Perfect.

"Alistair, it's funny how you have just now shown up after being lost for so long. However did Genie manage to find you two?" Jaffa pops an olive in his mouth and waits for an answer.

"Don't ask me, Genie's the one who did all the sleuthing." Street Rat turns the tables to me. Smart kid.

"What was your mother's name again and how did she die? Help jog my memory. I seem to be lacking details all of a sudden." Jaffa lights his cigarette and blows puffs of smoke into the air above him. He's relaxed back in his chair, as though his shit doesn't stink, and he has a right to speak at this table.

I watch Boo and Street Rat shift ever so slightly, obviously uncomfortable in answering probing questions about a history that isn't theirs.

"Enough!" Salvatore puts a stop to Jaffa and his unnecessary questions. "There's a time and place for that, and here is not the place. I'm here to discuss the fights and not dwell on the past." He shoots a look at Jaffa in warning. "Alistair, are you up to the task of more fights against the best men in the business?"

"Do I have a choice?" Street Rat takes a tentative sip of his whiskey and challenges Salvatore to say otherwise.

"Papa," Jaz's melodic voice interrupts the sudden tension. "What happens when I return to classes on campus? I can't have Genie following me around." She touches her Papa's arm and demands his attention.

"We'll enroll and watch over her." Boo offers his and Street Rat's services without thinking.

Street Rat slaps Boo in the arm and clears his throat. "What he means is, we're happy to be on campus and keep an eye on Jazlyn."

"No!" Jazlyn protests. "I'm not being fucking babysat!"

"Are you fucking kidding me?! You're going to let these two sewer rats watch over your daughter?" Jaffa slams his fist onto the table.

"What's wrong with us two sewer rats? Worried your little ticket will trade you in?" Boo clinks his glass to Street Rat's and takes a sip of the expensive whiskey.

"Papa!"

"It actually makes perfect sense to have these two there with her. They're more believable to be students than me." This was not how I expected the evening discussion to go. But it is in my favor to have these guys close at all times.

Salvatore glances around the table until his eyes land on Street Rat. "Anything happens to her, you're held accountable."

"Yes, sir." Street Rat nods before his gaze lands on Jaffa, who sits there fuming. "We'll make sure she's well taken care of." He winks at Jaffa to rile him up, and it works.

"Keep your filthy hands off her!" He slams his hands on the table and stands ready to start a fight, but I'm at his side at once.

"Calm the fuck down or I'll throw you out." I grip his arm to ensure he doesn't try anything stupid.

Jaz stands abruptly, her chair falling to the ground in her movement. She extends a finger toward Jaffa. "You don't get a say in who can and can't touch me. I don't give a fuck who you are to my Papa. I decide. And if I want these two to fuck me, then that's my choice!" Her breasts heave as her anger swirls in her like a hurricane.

"Sit the fuck down, Jazlyn," Salvatore orders, his disgust in her language shows in how he glares at Boo and Street Rat.

Jaz bends down and picks up her chair before sitting her ass back down in a huff. She knows better than anyone her Papa's tolerance for spoiled brat behavior is non-existent. My eyes slice to Boo as he sits in his chair and revels in the statement Jaz just made. If only she knew that the two guys she let fuck her are, in fact, the two sitting here eating up her anger and feasting on it until they get their hands on her again.

Jaffa pulls out of my grip and storms out of the private dining room before Salvatore can order him otherwise. His plan to be top dog is slowly unravelling right under his nose, and there's not a fucking thing he can do about it unless he does a one-eighty and changes his sleazy as fuck behavior toward Jaz.

I take my seat and place my napkin back on my lap when the wait staff delivers our food. Everyone sits in silence as the plates are placed in front of us. It smells delicious, and my stomach growls in appreciation. I have no idea who ordered what for us, but the pasta swirled in a neat circle on my plate makes my mouth water.

"Cheers to you and cheers to me, the best of friends we'll ever be, and if we ever disagree, fuck you and cheers to me." Boo holds his glass up in salute.

Street Rat nearly spits his drink out as everyone's eyes land upon Boo. Salvatore doesn't look too pleased, and I'm sure he is questioning his decision to let these two near his daughter as well as watch over her a college.

CHAPTER TEN

Jazlyn

The cold rain pelts against my skin as I scurry across the courtyard to my next class. This college is my only escape from my Papa and his overbearing ways, and now he's hired these two to watch over me as though I can't take care of myself. It irritates me more than I want it to. I'd never let on that Alistair and Abel are really fucking good eye candy though, and I see the way they stare at me. The way that their gazes trail over my skin as though they've seen every inch of me before. I'll never let on that I fantasize about them every night when I'm alone in bed and have my trusty Rabbit between my milky thighs as I fuck myself and imagine it's one of their cocks.

"What dirty things are circling in that pretty little head of yours?" Alistair's voice snakes over me. I turn in surprise and bump straight into his hard chest.

He catches me around the waist, pulling me possessively against his muscled abs, his hand pressing against my lower back just above my ass. I drink in his dangerous smirk, and there's something sinister that lurks behind his almost black eyes. A tightly guarded secret that he won't share for any price.

"Wouldn't you like to know." I press my hand against his chest to get a feel of his muscles and gently push at him to make him think I want to get away from him.

His hooded gaze snakes over me, and I glance up at his perfectly styled dark hair. He oozes old school gangster, a style only a few can carry with such sexiness. His grip around my waist gets tighter and brings back salacious memories of my night with those two guys. I bite my lip at the thought of ever seeing them again.

"I know that look, mafia princess," Alistair whispers against my ear.

"Don't call me that." Anger burns my throat, and I try to get out of his grip, but the struggle excites me, and desire pools between my legs as he holds me tight against his body.

"Don't like nicknames?" His eyes darken a shade, and he darts his tongue to moisten his lips.

I follow his every move when I feel a body press up behind me.

"You two started without me? My jealous ass is feeling left out." His voice brushes against the back of my neck and sends goosebumps to spread over my skin.

I turn my head to glance up at Abel. His sultry lips quirk up at the corner to reveal a sardonic grin full of promise. "You haven't missed anything. Alistair here was about to let me get to class before I'm late and lose marks for non-attendance."

"I'm pretty sure you were pouting about me calling you mafia princess." Alistair grins at Abel, and they share a private joke that I don't care enough to want to know about.

"Well, we better get your sexy little ass to class before you get into trouble." Abel steps back from me at the same time as Alistair. Their synchronized movements are unnerving.

I glance between them and shake my head at the thought of having them as babysitters. This is fucking ridiculous, but at least it has Armando off my back for today. My gaze slices to Abel when he falls in beside me as I make my way to my class through the drizzling rain. He's sexy as fuck and dressed impeccably right down to the Italian designer shoes. I can smell his masculine cologne as it mixes with the fresh rain, and it does stupid things to my insides. I need to control my thoughts around these two because I'm sure they can read minds or faces or some shit.

Alistair, ever the gentleman, opens the tutorial hall door and lets me enter first. I eye the room and head to the back to take a seat, purposefully finding a row with three empty seats together. They flank me when we finally settle in for the class.

"What are we taking today?" Abel leans into me and hands Alistair something from his pocket.

"Economics." I look at him and smile, knowing he'll be suffering through the whole hour and a half class.

"You're fucking kidding, right? Wake me up when it's over." Abel slinks down into his seat, rests his head against the backrest, and closes his eyes.

"My boy isn't into studying." Alistair snorts and reaches around my shoulder to slap the back of Abel's head. His closeness has my heart thudding in my chest, and I want him to leave his arm there, but he doesn't. He moves back into his seat and settles in for an hour and a half of a boring class.

———

"Hey, sleepy head, wake up. Class is over." I tap Abel on the shoulder, and he jerks up to a sitting position.

"Whose ass do I need to kick?" He glances around the room at the other students leaving before his gaze rests back on me.

"Let's get some caffeine into us. I'm so fucking tired after that." Alistair stands and yawns as he stretches.

I pack up my bag as they both wait for me. I could get used to this, their overbearing company is not as terrible as I first thought. "I know a coffee place." I skip past them and head toward the door when the lecturer calls my name. I stop and glance at the front of the room where the lecturer looms over his desk.

"A moment, please, Jazlyn." He removes his thick-rimmed glasses and places them on his desk.

I move across the room and stop about a foot away from his desk. Alistair and Abel stand behind me like body-guards. The lecturer has never once called me up to the front of the room for anything. He looks at the two behind me with wariness before he speaks.

"Your attention must remain on the class. If you're not interested in what I have to say, please feel free not to attend my classroom in future." He dismisses me with a wave of a hand.

I stare at him in confusion. "Excuse me. I have three pages of notes that prove I was listening."

"I can confirm that." Alistair attempts to help, but I glare back at him to shut up.

"And you are?" The lecturer eyes Alistair with disdain.

"Alistair Barber."

Something registers on the lecturer's face before he schools himself and ignores us completely before he grabs his bag and glasses and hurries out of the room.

"Well, that was weird." I glance at Alistair.

"My boy knows how to clear a room. Usually, it's from letting a rotten fart go in the middle of a meeting. True story," Abel chuckles and drapes his arm around my neck.

"Oh my God," I can't help but laugh as he leads me outside with Alistair behind us.

The rain has stopped, and the lecturer has disappeared into thin air. "Have you ever met him before?" I look up at Alistair.

"Swear on my mother's grave, I have never laid eyes on him." He holds up a hand, palm facing me.

He looks genuine in his response, and I wonder what the fuck the lecturer's issue is. Maybe this will keep him off my back. I know the lecturer knows about my family and who my Papa is, but I never expect anyone to treat me differently because of it. But being associated with Alistair might not be so bad after all.

"So, where's the coffee place?" Alistair scans the courtyard searching for something.

"It's over that way, through those two buildings, where the massive grass area is." I point in the direction they need to walk.

"You know you're coming with us, right?" Abel's arm tightens around my shoulders as he pulls me into him. "You're ours to watch over. We don't need your Papa removing our heads anytime soon."

"You don't need to follow me everywhere. Don't you have classes to attend too?"

"We signed up to all of yours," Alistair says matter of fact.

Of course, they did, Papa wouldn't have had it any other way, and the Dean would have bent over backwards to make it happen.

CHAPTER ELEVEN

Street Rat

The fucking mafia, I think to myself, looking in the floor to ceiling mirror. Who needs a mirror that big. I'm six-foot-one, and what am I looking at above my head? Absolutely nothing. I'm also not a huge fan of these clothes, even if the material feels like heaven on my skin.

I give myself a once over, from the black muscle shirt, tucked into a pair of plaid dress pants rolled at the ankles, with white sneakers. My hair is slicked back and not even one hair is out of place, and I pair the outfit with a silver Rolex.

"Looking good," Boo says, striding into the room, dressed much the same, except switch the sneakers out from a pair of Italian leather lace-ups. If anyone was made for this world, it's him.

"Thanks, I feel like a fish out of water. This isn't me."

"Because here you are Alistair Barber, descendant of Francesca Cattaneo, who married Charles Cattaneo the second. Which if you ask me was a marriage doomed from the start. And don't forget Francesca's great, great granddaughter was Alissa Barber, Salvatore's first love. I can understand why Genie wants to find out what happened to his family. It was a bloodbath, they picked them off one by one until no one was left. Which makes me wonder how he himself survived."

I shrug. "That's not our problem."

"What is your plan, do you even have one?" he asks.

"Fucks me, I wanted to get close to her, and it's messing with my head. I don't get close to people, but I felt this connection."

Boo snorts. "That connection was your dick getting excited because it hadn't fucked in a while. Fuck man, I thought you learned that when you were a teenager. It also could be a UTI."

"Fuck off," I reply, and he laughs. "Once I realized they were mafia, it was too late. We are in this neck deep, so we may as well get something out of it."

"And in the meantime, you have another fight coming up. There has to be a way out of it."

"I don't see how; I killed his star fighter."

"Good point, I'm sure we will think of something unless you get yourself killed first."

I laugh, that isn't going to happen, where we come from you learn to fight as soon as you learn to walk. We have no other option. I also had the help of Lady Trey. People only see a dude in a dress, but damn, she is the best fucking street fighter on our block. She can kick your ass in heels before you could even blink.

"Let's go, her class starts soon."

Boo nods and starts to complain about why someone

would do an aerobics class early in the morning, that the only exercise anyone should do before nine is fucking, and I have to agree.

Boo grabs the keys and throws them to me, we head out into the garage, and the purple 1970s dodge charger is waiting for us. I'm not into cars as much as Boo is, but even I can appreciate a beauty like this.

The drive to campus isn't long, the thumb of the engine vibrates through the steering wheel, and I feel fucking powerful as I pull into a spot next to a red fucking sports car, and Armando leans casually against the bonnet.

"Gentleman," he nods as we exit the car. "Beautiful day isn't it."

"Sure is, I can say I'm very excited about this aerobics class and the skintight booty shorts."

I shake my head at Boo, he is pushing Armando's buttons, and I don't blame him, the guy needs to pull the huge stick out from his ass.

"You haven't won her over yet, I wouldn't get too cocky because I'm onto you."

I laugh, he might think he is slick, but this isn't my first rodeo. "You mean your little lackey that has been following us around. He should really stick to booking your appointments and wiping your ass."

Armando steps away from his car, and I step closer to him. "I will find out who you are, and what you're up to. Then I will expose the truth to Salvatore, and we will see how far you get."

"Good luck with that, Champ," Boo says, sliding his body between us. I take a step back and keep my eyes trained on Armando, he is a slimy fucker.

"I'll be watching you," he says, and Boo laughs.

"As long as you capture my good side," Boo jokes.

Armando huffs and gets back into his car, rolling down the window. "Tell Jaz I will be back to pick her up after her first class."

Boo and I walk up to the aerobics class that is apparently outside this morning, and thank God, the class is taking place near the small coffee cart.

"Now this is what I'm talking about," Boo jokes. Jaz stands next to her friend Raj, who looks like he is really into this class. Jaz on the other hand is present but not really overly into it.

"I'm going to see if they need a hand. Can you get me one of those caramel coffee things with the cream on top?"

I nod, and he runs up to join the class. Jaz puts her hands across her chest in a defensive stance, but he must say something to her that lightens the mood because she shakes her head, drops her arms, and laughs at him.

Genie is leaning against the brick wall beside the coffee cart, his eyes trained on Jaz. "You should make a move."

He glances over at me but quickly puts his attention back on her. "I thought you wanted her."

"I do," I say, leaning against the wall beside him. "Did you not learn to share in school?"

He snorts at me, the idea of sharing a girl with Boo makes sense. I hate being tied down, the feeling suffocates me. The idea of monogamy doesn't make sense to Boo, he is a free spirit. He just wants to love everyone.

"Sharing your coloring pencils with your peers and sharing a woman are vastly different things."

"They don't have to be, we all lead lives that could

JAYE PRATT & MELINDA TERRANOVA

potentially bring harm to anyone we get close with. Why would I not want my best friend to help me protect her, or when I have a job, I know that she is being looked after. And shouldn't love be infinite?"

Genie snorts and elbows me in the ribs. "You're just repeating what he said."

He nods toward Boo, and I laugh. "I sure am, but for me, it's complicated. And is there anything hotter than watching a girl be fucked from both ends? I think not."

"I can imagine the appeal," he says casually.

"One coffee, black, and a caramel macchiato." The girl gives me a nod. She most likely just heard our entire conversation.

"Why are you here anyway? Salvatore is happy for us to watch Jaz."

Genie sighs. "Because Salvatore didn't ask me to watch her, Armando did. I work for him when it comes to Jazlyn."

I quirk a brow at him. "So, are you spying on us too?"

"Would I have given you a new identity if I was going back to him with information? Armando can't be trusted."

The young girl comes around and hands me my coffee. "It's on the house Mr. Barber."

She winks at me and walks away, with a little sway in her hips.

"What was that about?" I ask Genie.

"Perks of being associated with the Bianchi family."

A girly shriek has my attention back to Boo and Princess, Boo is, he is currently pretending to dry hump Raj from behind. I think it's supposed to be some kind of dance move, but you can never be too sure with Boo. He likes to fuck, and he has no gender preference. There was this one time that he tried to slip a finger in my ass, and it was all kinds of weird.

"Is your friend bi?"

I shake my head no. "Boo just does whatever Boo wants to do."

He nods, I turn to face him. "Why are you interested?"

"I can't say that I'm not interested," he replies.

I know he is interested in Jaz, I can see it when he looks at her, so he must be bi, considering he asked me if Boo was.

"I wouldn't be stepping on your toes if I did make a move?"

I snort. "Definitely not stepping on any toes. I feel like it's some rule somewhere that best friends don't fuck each other, we share and sometimes touch and that's always fun."

"You good to take Jaz to class?" he asks.

"Of course I am."

Genie pushes off the brick wall, and I follow a few steps behind. I fall back slightly when he approaches Boo, walks straight up behind him, leans in, and whispers something in his ear. Boo turns around, and he finds me. His eyes making sure that I'm okay with him leaving, I nod, and his shit-eating grin all but shouts, 'I'm going to get my ass fucked.'

I know Boo likes to bottom, I hear the stories, and Genie looks like a man who would take control. I close the distance between Jaz and me.

"Is that for me?" she asks, and I shrug. It's not like Boo needs it now. Handing her the caramel crap that was for Boo, she looks toward the parking lot as Genie and Boo slip into the black Range Rover.

"Where are they going?" she asks.

I shrug, it's none of her business, but Raj answers, "They're going to suck each other's cocks, baby girl."

She gasps. "Are they gay? I swear Genie is straight."

Raj laughs. "Genie is bisexual, how did you miss it? Last year he was boning that security guard your brother hired, come to think of it he vanished pretty fast."

"And what about you, are you bisexual?"

"Princess, I love eating ass, but it needs to be attached to a pussy."

She squeezes her legs together, and her cheeks flush a pretty pink.

"Well, all this talk of sex has me hot and bothered, I need to go find a jock who is still finding his sexuality to relieve some stress."

With that, he flirts off in the direction of the sports center.

Jaz and I walk to her economics class, she finds her seat, and I take the one beside her and stretch my arm out behind her seat. I expect her to move it away, but she doesn't.

Who would have thought economics would be so fucking boring. Critical thinking skills, what a load of crap. I will give you critical thinking when you have to run for your life. I sit through the lecture and keep my mouth shut.

Fifteen minutes before the class ends, I see Armando standing outside of the classroom. Jaz and I sit near a big window, right at the back of the room.

"I have to take a leak, do not leave the room. Your future husband is waiting outside."

She nods and doesn't stop listening to the professor. I

have a plan, one that could get me killed but also totally worth it.

Jumping up from my seat, I unclip the window lock and open it ever so slightly before I slip from the room.

"Lecture finishes in about ten minutes, you have this from here."

Armando just nods and leans against the wall with his legs crossed at the ankles. I rush from the building and race straight to the car, sliding into the driver's seat, I turn the key, and it rumbles to life.

Luckily the Economics classroom backs onto the large grass area. There are a handful of students leaning against a tree, and they eye me wearily when I drive up off the road and onto the grass, then I pull the car right up to the window. Fuck, Genie may kill me for denting this thing, but I don't care. I leave the car running and climb up onto the roof, which makes me just tall enough to see into the classroom. Slowly I push the window up, and I am almost able to reach in and touch her.

"Psst...psst, Princess," I whisper.

She turns, and her mouth opens and then shuts again.

"What are you doing?" she asks.

I smirk. "I'm saving you from your fate."

She shakes her head. "Or would you rather go with Armando."

She looks toward the closed door and back to me. "Screw it," she says with a laugh, picking up her stuff and shoving it into her backpack.

Once she is at the window, she hesitates. "I don't know if I can do this."

"It's not that far, I will help you down."

"Miss Bianchi, what are you doing?"

"Shit, help me out."

She climbs through the window, sitting on the window ledge. "Do you trust me, Princess?"

"No, I don't trust anyone," she replies, narrowing her eyes at me.

"Good," I reply as she slips down from where she is sitting, and I catch her by the waist. She falls into me, and it takes me a second to help her with her balance. She looks up at me and smiles. I lean in and focus on her mouth.

"Jazlyn, what the hell are you doing?" Armando demands, hanging out of the window. "Get back here right now."

Jaz flips him off before I jump from the roof, she follows me down as we scramble into the car and put my foot on the gas, fishtailing my way across the grass as the sweet sound of her laughter fills the car.

CHAPTER TWELVE

Boo

Genie is all hard lines and seriousness. So, when he walked up behind me and whispered,

"Your ass is mine, let's go," I was surprised.

I never would have guessed he was into guys; I know for a fact he wants to fuck Jaz. The lust that burns in his eyes is equal to Street Rat's. This chick has so many men falling at her feet, and I would be one of them because I'm an opportunist, and I won't say no to a good time.

He drove us to a dingy motel off the highway, and once he paid for the room, there was no wasting time.

The second we walked through the door, I stripped out of my clothes. Men who look like that don't come around often, and something tells me this man has something long, thick, and hard between his legs.

His eyes drop to my cock, and I smirk at him. He closes the distance between us and wraps his large hand around my throat in a bruising grip. In any normal situation, I would fight back, but this has my cock hard as steel and excitement burning deep in my stomach. He leans in, and his lips smash against mine, but he is gentle. This man takes what he wants, and I fucking love that. I love being a little Boo ragdoll. His tongue dominates its way into my mouth, forcing its way past my lips. Moaning against his mouth, he pulls back.

"Get on your knees and show me why it was worth pulling your ass off the street."

Fuck, you don't have to ask me twice. Dropping to my knees, I unbuckle his belt and have his zipper down in seconds. His hard cock stares me in the face, and I lick my lips.

"Fuck," I say when I see the Jacob's ladder and top ladder lining his cock. Now this is going to be fun. Excitement dances in my gut. Fuck the head job, he can bend me over and maneuver me like a pretzel for all I care.

Licking my lips to make way for his size, I lean forward and wrap my lips around his head, running my tongue along his slit. He takes charge, gripping the back of my head, and thrusts hard into my mouth, forcing his way down my throat, I relax my throat and hum around his length.

"That's it, take it all like a good little slut."

My insides clench at his words, and excitement swirls in the pit of my stomach. I'm so fucking turned on, my own cock is rock hard, pre cum making a sticky mess against my skin. With one hand pressed to his abs while he thrusts into my throat, using me for his own pleasure, I wrap my hand around my aching cock and stroke myself as my eyes roll into the back of my head.

"Don't you fucking dare come until I tell you to. Both hands up here."

I groan around him at the loss of friction. He abruptly pulls out, and I look up at him in disbelief. He smirks down at me and runs a thumb across my swollen lips, then slides his thumb into my mouth. With a moan, I close my lips around it and suck, twirling my tongue around it.

"On the bed and spread your legs."

He steps back, watching me push up from my knees. His gaze burns into me, and I do as he asks, moving from the floor and up onto the bed, lying on my back with my legs spread.

When I'm in position, he moves closer, kneeling on the bed and moving up closer to me. His hands fall either side of me, and he leans down, smashing his lips to mine, biting my bottom lips between his teeth before he pulls back and releases it.

He moves back and uses his forearm to push my legs up in the air and leans down and spits against my ass. If he doesn't put his cock in me now, there is a good possibility that I will start fighting back and sit my ass on jeweled up cock and route myself on it. I'm so wound up, I'm ready to burst.

With my legs thrown over his shoulders, he palms his cock, running it up and down my crack, before lining it up and sliding the head inside. I moan as he slowly slides in, and my eyes widen as the first barbell rubs across my prostate. He bellows out a laugh; the asshole knew this was going to happen.

"Fuck, stop for a second, I'm going to come already."

He shakes his head no and thrusts hard inside me. A

few things happen simultaneously: my eyes roll in the back of my head, my cock feels like it's never been harder, and my stomach tightens as white ropes of cum squirt up my chest, and my body shakes from the over stimulation. Genie pulls out, and I'm momentarily limp. He flips me over onto my stomach, and his calloused hands grip my hips and pull my ass into the air before slamming back into me.

"Your ass is so fucking tight; you take me so well. Be a good boy and scream for me."

Jesus motherfucking Christ, I have never been called a good boy before, but his words have me melting into a puddle and panting at the same time. The sensation of the barbells on the top and bottom have me screaming his name so loud it ricochets off the walls. Come just starts leaking out of me. I don't even think it stops, and I don't know if that is possible, but my orgasm feels like it's just keeps tipping over the edge as he expertly rotates his hips behind me. His low grunts tell me he is getting closer to filling me.

Genie's phone starts to vibrate, and he thrusts harder and harder, chasing his release. He thrusts forward one last time, all the way to the hilt, where he spasms a little with small thrusts until he flops on top of me, reaching over to grab his phone.

"What," he barks, still inside me. "Fine, I will be right there."

He pushes up, and his flaccid cock slips out of me. He pads across the room and walks into the bathroom. Not wanting to be left behind, I roll and spring up off the bed and walk into the bathroom where he is already showering.

"Go get dressed, my cum stays inside you."

I smirk and chuckle at him, possessive motherfucker. "Who called?" I ask, looking at my reflection in the mirror. Fuck, my hair is crazy, and everyone will know I was just fucked. I turn the tap on and dip my hand under the water and run my hand through my hair.

"Armando. Jaz and Street Rat gave him the slip an hour ago, and he can't find them. Jaz has a wedding dress fitting."

"I thought she didn't have to marry him."

He sticks his head out from behind the flimsy shower curtain. "She still has to be married by the time she is twenty-one, so she still needs the dress."

"Fair enough, hurry up and wash that hot ass. I know where he would have taken her."

He pops his head back behind the curtain and then steps straight out. My eyes rake over his toned body covered in tattoos, and I imagine licking each and every one. Fuck, Armando ruining my good time.

"As much as the way you're looking at me right now and I want to choke you with my cock again, if Jaz isn't doing what Salvatore wants, I have to find her."

"Rain check then, maybe next time we can sandwich a certain princess between us."

I wiggle my brows at him, and he laughs. Come on, it's not a horrible idea. Street Rat might murder me in my sleep if I don't include him.

Directing Genie toward Kingston Village, I make him take an off road just before the turn off. Street Rat and I would come out here all the time. The rock pools are beautiful, and the hiking track is magical. A great place to bring someone to kill them or fuck them. Sneaky little motherfucker isn't going to kill her, he is mildly obsessed with her.

We drive until there is no road left, and lo and behold, the purple Charger is under a tree. Genie parks next to it, and we jump out of the Range Rover.

"Lead the way," he says, and I have to take a guess which track he would take her on. There are three, but I hedge a guess that since they left from class, Jaz would still be in the heels that she was wearing, and he would have been kind enough to use the shortest one.

"Let's go this way."

Genie walks in step with me, and we walk in comfortable silence.

"So, what's your deal anyway?" I ask. The comfortable silence needed to end. Siska says that I love the sound of my own voice.

"What do you mean?"

"Just, if the Barbers are your family and you have all this wealth, why hide behind the Façade of being personal security to the mafia?"

"Because no one will openly come out and tell me they killed my entire family. And being close to Salvatore and even Armando, I go with them to meetings, I overhear a lot of things, and I have made connections with other bodyguards."

"I suppose, but I doubt anyone who knows anything is going to talk. Whoever took out an entire family isn't going to be gossiping about it in front of anyone."

"Good point."

We keep walking, and I start to regret not showering. It was hot as fuck him wanting his cum to stay inside me, but fuck me, my ass is damn chaffing from all this walking. Finally, I see the damn clearing, and just beyond the trees is a water hole; it's picture perfect and where Street Rat likes to go and think. Genie and I walk side by side, but he puts his arm out to stop me just before we step out into the open.

"Ouch, man."

"Shhh," he whispers and points. Street Rat has his head between Jaz's legs.

"Fuck, Alistair, just there, don't stop."

We stand there and watch as Jaz explodes on Street Rat's face. He stands quickly before she can recover and moves her hands above her head, her back still pressed against a tree and her skirt pulled up around her waist. He uses his free hand to unbuckle his pants and pull his cock out.

"Want me to cum in that ass again?" Genie whispers in my ear. Fuck, when did he move behind me? I find myself nodding. I drop my pants around my ankles and bend, leaning my hand against the tree in front of me. My eyes never leave Jaz and Street Rat. Genie pushes inside of me.

"I never took you as someone who likes to watch others fuck."

He chuckles. "And I bet you didn't think that I liked to fuck men in the ass either."

"Touche."

My eyes roll in the back of my head as he slides all the way in. This man has a fucking fantastic cock, with the barbells lined all the way down, and I almost cum at the sensation.

I wrap my free hand around my cock as he thrusts into me. He rests one hand on my hip, and the other wraps around my throat.

Our bodies slap together, and I bite down on my tongue to silence myself as Jaz's mewls fill the air.

The death grip I have on my own cock and the noises from Jaz have me coming on the ground in front of me. Genie softly growls from behind me, dropping the hand around my neck, and grips both sides of my hips and thrusts deep, spilling himself inside me again.

"Time to make our presence known," he says, pulling out of me and tucking himself away. I snort.

"Dude, he knows we are here."

Jaz crumbles around Street Rat's cock, and he shouts her name on his release just as we step out of the clearing, and I clap my hands.

"Now that was fucking hot. Never in my life did I think that I would get a ten-inch cock in my ass while watching the princess get fucked, but here we are."

Jaz narrows her eyes at me, and Street Rat laughs. Genie doesn't say anything, I follow his line of sight, and the princess has her foo foo out for us all to appreciate. Damn, she has a pretty pussy.

"Can I lick it?"

"No," she snaps, pulling her skirt back down.

I shrug. "No harm in asking. Big man here would love to suck his come from your coochie."

Her eyes go wide, and she looks at Genie. She doesn't protest, I see the way she is thinking about it. "Come on, Princess, soon you will be married to mister stick up his ass, and at least you can look back at today and remember getting fucked while two men fucked to get off watching you, and then your bodyguard sucking the cum out of you."

"Fuck it," Genie says just loud enough that I can hear him. He steps forward and doesn't stop until he is right in front of her. She gives him a slight nod, and that's all he needs. He drops to his knees, and his head goes straight between her thighs, and he hooks one of her legs over his shoulder.

Street Rat and I join them, standing either side. He goes straight to her blouse and slips the thin strap down her shoulder, her pretty tits as visible through the camisole she wears underneath. He leans down and bites her nipple through the material.

I run a finger down her arm, testing to see if she wants me to touch her. She doesn't know we have fucked before, and I don't know if my touch alone would make her take notice. She moans louder and doesn't push me away, so I keep going until I squeeze one of her ass cheeks between my fingers.

Let's really make this interesting. I move down, and Genie side-eyes me, but I show him my fingers and smirk. He moves up to focus on her clit while I bury two fingers into her wetness and slide my best friend's cum to her ass.

She freezes, and Street Rat whispers something into her ear, making her body relax. I push one finger in, and her mewls spur me on, pushing in a second finger.

Her orgasm must be close because her screams of pleasure get louder as we work her into a frenzy from all angles.

"Oh, fuck!" she screams, and her ass clenches around my tattooed fingers. I watch as she squirts all over Genie's face. That lucky motherfucker.

"Boys, we have a squirter, and fuck, I'm hard again."

Genie stands and wipes his face with his hand; I have

never wanted to lick a man's face so much before in my life. I grab him by the back of the neck, and he smirks at me. I lick down the side of his face and press my lips to his. The taste of her sweetness dances on his tongue, and I moan into his mouth.

We pull apart, and Jaz looks at us with a mix of excitement and lust and a little bit of something I can't place.

"Holy shit," she whispers.

"Holy shit, alright," I repeat, and she laughs.

"Please, can we tell Jaffa?" she giggles.

"No," Genie demands. "He will have my head, Jaz. I can't lose this job."

He goes to turn his back on us, but Jaz reaches out and grabs his hand.

"Hey, I was only joking. I hate him, and I wouldn't risk your job or your head."

He nods and tells her that we have to go, and she agrees because she doesn't want Jaffa to go to her father. Once we are back at the cars, Genie takes Jaz to her dress fitting, and Street Rat and I head back to the mansion. I secretly hope that Genie comes back with her later for some more fun. A man can only hope...right?

CHAPTER THIRTEEN

Jaffa

"Fuck! Shit! Fuck!" I shout and swipe all the paperwork off my desk. Frustration festers in me at the thought of those two slimy fucks getting away with infiltrating the Bianchi family and taking what belongs to me.

I glare at the walls that feel like they're closing in on me. The suffocation of this dingy office in the back of the restaurant has my nerves ramping up. I swear these walls have ears and whisper stolen secrets, telling tales of corruption and betrayal. This family is only loyal to their own. If one of us non-blood members steps one foot out of line, Salvatore gives no remorse in removing us.

"Oh, fuck. He's cracked. Calm your tits." Isaac settles himself on the leather sofa against the wall and sucks on his cigar.

Isaac is my eyes and ears, and the most trusted out of all the men who work for me. I give him an order, and he carries it out. No questions asked. He's loyal as fuck and does as he's told. There's nothing more important to corrupt fuckers like us. We need that one person who we can rely on through all the bullshit this line of work throws at us, and know at the end of the day, they will choose you over anything else. I pay him well for his servitude, and he delivers day in day out.

"Those fuckers are not who they say they are. I know it. I can feel it in my veins that they are up to something, but I can't for the life of me figure out what. That's where your next assignment comes into play."

Isaac leans forward, his eyes settling on me. "You want me to spy on them?" He looks at me in confusion.

"That's exactly what you're going to do, and you're going to do it until I'm proven right. That these fuckers aren't who Genie says they are." I chew on the inside of my mouth as I contemplate doing the dirty work myself to reap the satisfaction of catching them out.

"Why the sudden interest in who these two men are?"

I narrow my eyes at him. "They're threatening to take what is rightfully mine," I growl out of frustration.

Isaac chuckles. "Isn't it now up to Jazlyn to decide who she is married off to? I'm pretty sure she's not picking you."

"Fuck you." My anger rages in my veins as the thought of her slipping out of my fingers becomes more of a reality.

"A little touchy there. Get a grip. Use your charms to lure her in. Give her a false sense of hope that you're really a good man that will love her and dote on her spoiled princess ass." Isaac blows cigar smoke out in rings above his head.

I eye him and wonder what brings a man to carry out the dirty work I dish out to him. What the fuck went wrong in his childhood for him to grow up and be happy to be this? It dawns on me that I am nothing more than him in the scheme of things. I too just do as Salvatore says.

"You just concentrate on taking down these slimy fuckers. Follow them and record what you can. Report back to me when you discover something worthwhile. I'll worry about how to lure Jazlyn into a false sense of hope that I'm a good man." I grab my tumbler and throw back the expensive malt whiskey. The mellow burn down my throat warms my cold heart just enough for me to believe I can put on an act of being a decent man and showing her how a princess is meant to be treated.

"And if Salvatore finds out?" Isaac takes in another lungful of cigar before he settles against the back of the sofa again with a look of contemplation on his otherwise serene face.

"Fuck Salvatore. He'll be kissing my fucking feet when I uncover this bullshit."

"Whatever you say, boss. But if it all goes to shit, I'm not taking the downfall." Isaac turns to gaze at the door behind him.

The jiggle of the door handle has my attention, and I indicate to Isaac to not say another word about my plans as the door creaks open. In waltzes my prized possession. Her eyes are the color of the ocean on a nice day, and her icy hair cascades over her tanned shoulders, begging for me to wrap the long locks around my fists and pull.

Men fall to their knees at the sight of her, their weakness is her power. She knows the effect she has on men, and although she plays the sweet card well, I know she is anything but the sweetness she portrays. Jazlyn is her father's daughter. Cunning and ruthlessness flows in her veins, and any man that thinks they can cross her wind up begging for their life. I know I need to play this game right. To ensure I end up with my prize. I need to show Jazlyn that I can be the man she wants. The man she needs to stand beside her in this mob world. The man she finally chooses.

"Jazlyn." I nod to acknowledge her presence. I grant her a smile worthy of an Oscar in itself.

She hesitates before she takes another step into the room. "Boys." She seats herself beside Isaac and stares at him as she adjusts herself on the sofa. "What riveting things are we discussing?"

"Your father's latest business dealings." I lean back in the plush leather office chair and feel the hardness of my dick press against the zipper of my suit pants. Just the sight of her in her tight leather mini, with her long legs on display, has my dick jump to attention. What I wouldn't give to grip her by the throat, bend her over this desk, and fuck her into oblivion.

"Found your suitor yet?" Isaac teases as he blows cigar smoke toward Jaz.

I could fucking put a bullet hole in his head right at this point. I glare at him, but the fucker's gaze is trained on her.

"No one worthy." She watches him carefully, and her eyes flicker to me.

"What about Armando? I hear he's a changed man." Isaac's eyes crinkle at the corners as he chuckles to himself.

Before I can get a word in, Jazlyn's mouth twitches into a sly smirk. She watches me intently, and I see something different in the way she looks at me. Something behind that mask of hers that is always present when she's watching me.

Almost as though she's hiding her true feelings and keeping her desires to herself.

"If all else fails and I'm forced to marry you, at least one day I will have the power to get rid of you from this family for good." Her words flick out like a snake strike, but the conviction behind them is weak. She can play this hatred game all she wants, but I'm no fool and neither is she.

I grab my chest over my heart and feign being hurt. "Your words have such an effect on my feelings, Jazlyn. You are as ruthless as your father." I grin at her and see her features soften at my playfulness.

She can't stop the smirk that dances across her sultry lips, and the feeling that it elicits within me has me questioning myself. "You have no feelings, Armando, other than those of bloodshed." She tilts her head and waits for my response.

My name on her lips makes my dick twitch. Rarely does she call me by my name, and here I am feeling like a fucking teenager. This verbal insult exchange is something new too. Our usual interactions are filled with her disdain and my aggression. "Nothing wrong with a bit of bloodshed where warranted. What can I say, seeing people bleed turns me on." I purposely dart my tongue out and moisten my lips. And I get her, hook, line, and sinker. Her gaze follows my every move, and I see the fire in her belly as it warms her cold eyes.

"Okay, I'm out of here. You two archenemies carry on with your fucked flirting." Isaac stands, takes one last glance at me, and gives me a sly wink before he exits and leaves the two of us alone.

I watch his retreating figure and hope he finds out

something about those two slimeballs, and soon. I need them out of the picture and for things to return back to my original plan. But right now, my attention is stolen with the beauty sitting in front of me. I watch her, and she watches me. Both of us unsure how to proceed with this new and uncharted area laid out before us. I see the rise and fall of her breasts as she sits poised in her chair.

"Was there something you needed, Jazlyn?" I say her name with purpose, my voice low and husky.

I watch the bob of her throat as she swallows and picture my hand around it as I ram my cock into her. "Papa asked me to check if you're attending the gala and if he needs to organize a driver for you. We both know he just wanted me to come down here as he's still determined to pair us off." She pouts, and it's adorable.

Her disdain for me has weakened. I can sense it from the way her lip curls into a dazzling grin and the way she fights her need to show me she hates me. I climb out of my chair and skirt the desk until I hover over her and place my hands on the arm rests and cage her in. She shifts slightly, and I know my closeness is having the desired effect on her. I can see that she wants to touch me but stops herself. I grant her a salacious smile. Not my usual predatory grin but one I am having a hard time keeping on my face. A smile that shows her that I can be the kind of man she wants.

I lean in closer until my lips skim her delicate jawline, and I see the shiver of desire snake over her skin. "I wouldn't miss it," I whisper seductively, ensuring my lips brush against her with every word.

"Jazlyn, it's time to go." Genie steps through the door and watches me carefully as I straighten up.

Jaz stands slowly out of the seat and fixes her skirt. My eyes roam over her long, luscious legs, and I can sense Genie watching me, gauging my sudden change in behavior.

"I'll see you at the gala if not before." I raise my eyebrows at her and let my gaze settle on her beautiful face.

She doesn't say anything else to me before she exits the office with Genie right behind her, but not before he shoots me a warning look.

CHAPTER FOURTEEN

Jazlyn

Genie leans against the wall and watches as I do my make up. Things have changed between us since he had his head between my legs, and I can't say I hate it. He smirks every time I look at him.

"So, I see you took my advice."

I place my lipstick back down onto the tray and swivel around in my chair.

"And what advice is that?"

He pushes off the wall and stalks closer to me. I can't stop my eyes from caressing every inch of him. He looks fuckable in his tuxedo. These events are fancy as fuck, and the only plus I see to them is the gorgeous eye candy staring back at me. What is the Gala for? Good question. Some bored mafia wife has probably set it up to save the turtles or some shit.

"To get close to Armando, he is up to something."

Genie leans down and squats down in front of me, his

hands resting on my knees until he slides my dress up my legs and pushes them apart.

"I could say the same about you, Alistair, and Abel. Everyone is up to something. It's a dog-eat-dog world. Everyone has secrets."

"And what secrets are you hiding?" he asks, pressing a kiss to my inner thigh.

"If I tell you, it's no longer a secret."

He chuckles against my skin, and spreading my legs more, he leans in and breathes in against my pussy, sending shivers down my spine.

"Is your secret that you liked what happened the other day and you want to be fucked by three men?"

I laugh. "That isn't a secret, though I don't plan to tell my father. Your face is too pretty to be blown off."

He moves the material aside, and I can feel his breath against my bare pussy lips. Fuck, I need him to touch me.

"Tell me, Princess, what is one of your secrets?"

His tongue runs ever so lightly against my skin. I want him to push it past my lips and deep into my pussy, but he doesn't.

"Fine, I want to fuck Armando. I want him to fuck me the way his attitude is against me, but if I cross the line, he will want more."

"I don't know, I think that you should go for what you want."

"I think that you should take your own advice."

Genie laughs from between my legs and then pops his head out and smiles at me. "I think you're right, and just know that I'm putting my hat in the ring as a suitor. Fuck it." My mouth falls open in shock, my father would never allow me to marry my bodyguard. "I'm not who you think I am."

I quickly jump from my chair and reach under my table, but Genie is on me before I can pull the gun out. We have them hidden all over the house. He pins me to the table, using his entire body weight. "I'm not here to hurt you, so I would appreciate it if you didn't shoot me. My mother was murdered, and I'm trying to find out who killed her."

"And what if that was my father?"

"It wasn't, I ruled him out before coming to work for him. I will tell him when the time is right."

I sigh and nod. "I won't shoot you, but you do realize there is a possibility that he will? He hates being deceived."

"I do, but I have a plan. Please tell me that I can trust you with this."

"I won't tell anyone; you have my word."

A knock at the door has Genie leap off me, and I sit down and pick up my lipstick.

"Come in."

My brother pops his head in, and he scans the room, narrowing his eyes at Genie. "Father had some business to attend to and asked me to tell you that he will meet you at the Gala."

I nod, what else can I do? He is mafia, and that is code for he probably has a body to deal with. "Thank you, Romeo. Genie can drive me."

Romeo smiles and shuts the door behind himself. I think he forgets that I'm almost twenty-one and not a child anymore. Having a boy in my room isn't something that I was ever allowed to do. Shit, if it was anyone else other than Genie, they would probably have a bullet straight through their skull.

My phone vibrates, and a video message comes through from Raj. I click on it and roll my eyes. He is at the Gala already, rubbing shoulders with the mafia wives.

"A raincheck on eating your pussy?"

I look up at him and nod. "Maybe, unless someone else beats you to it."

I wink and try and be seductive, fuck. I have never had to try before, what was the point when I knew Jaffa was my endgame. Sure, I hooked up with guys secretly, ones who didn't know who I was or men with a death wish. Now, though, I have options. How the hell will I be able to pick when there isn't enough time to get to know any of them on that kind of level?

"Do I seem like the kind of man who cares? I ate your cunt after I fucked a man and after you had just fucked a man."

I squeeze my knees together at the thought, fuck. Who am I and what have I done with Jazlyn? Don't get me wrong, I love sex as much as the next person, but three at once? I wish I had some kind of plan, but I don't. I like them so it seems, and the sex is so good, better than good.

Genie ushers me out of the room and down to the garage where he is parked. Usually Papa likes me to ride with him so we arrive as a family, but I would much prefer to drive with Genie, he is much better to look at.

The drive over is fairly quiet, but I don't trust myself

with this man right now. I want to jump him, and the night hasn't even started yet, and he smells so fucking good. After a tense ride, Genie pulls up to my father's building, and there is a line of cars before us. He slowly creeps up, and when it's finally our turn, Genie climbs out of the Range Rover and stalks around to open my door. The valet waits patiently until Genie throws the car keys into his hands before jumping in and moving it from the lineup of other cars waiting to be parked. Genie slinks his arms through mine, and we walk the red carpet. These events can be ridiculous, so much glitz and glam, and for what, for the mafia to all be in one room at one time. Seems like a great way to pluck off your enemies if you ask me.

My breath catches in my throat when we walk in through the glass doors. The room is lined with fairy lights and over the top table decorations with dripping Diamante ornaments. But that isn't what catches my attention.

Alistair, Abel, and Armando are all watching me intently. The heat in their gaze sends butterflies to my stomach, and I feel giddy. Something has changed with Armando in the last few days. It's like instead of knowing I have no choice but to marry him and he can treat me like shit, he now realizes that he has competition, and he is coming to compete for me. Is it wrong that I like the idea of these men all wanting me? Does it make me sound like a slut? Fuck yes! Do I care? Fuck no. Why shouldn't I get what I want, I'm Jazlyn Bianchi, and Bianchi's take what they want, and they don't give a fuck about the consequences.

"What's running through that pretty head?" Genie whispers in my ear, and I chuckle.

"Wouldn't you want to know."

"I already know, Princess. You are imagining Alistair's face buried between your thighs and Abel's thick cock in your ass, while I fuck him as Armando watches."

"I wasn't thinking exactly that, but I am now. Fuck, Genie, we have hours here, and now I will be wet between my legs all night."

"Just say the word, and I will lick you clean, baby."

"Shh," I chastise. "And since when did you get so forward?"

"Since I realized that I have one shot to win you over before someone else steals you away, and I have to watch you from a distance."

We finally reach the three men who haven't stopped watching me, Abel smirks at me. "What has you all hot and bothered?"

"I think you should be asking who," Alistair replies.

I look up and lock eyes with Jaffa, wondering how he will respond, because he isn't the kind of man that stands around and waits, he takes what he wants. His family is just as ruthless as mine, it's the reason my father agreed to us being wed. A whole bunch of shit if you ask me. We are in an age where we should be able to marry for love and not what's in the best interest of our family.

"Whoever it is, I will make you forget they even existed," Armando adds with a flirty wink. Seriously, the man is fucking beautiful, and he knows it. A wink from him is enough that any woman would drop to her knees and beg to suck his cock.

"That's some big shoes to fill, Jaffa. I'm not sure a man such as yourself can deliver."

Taunting him is my favorite pastime. He takes a step forward and wraps his hand around the back of my neck and pulls me in close to him so he can lean down and whisper into my ear.

"Don't tempt me, baby girl, I will fuck you right here in front of the entire room, and your father wouldn't do a god damned thing about it, and anyone who tried to stop me will end up with a bullet in their fucking head."

His hand touches my thigh, and he moves it around the front of my dress and over my pussy, sending shivers through my body.

"This cat and mouse game that we play is fun, but when you fuck a man like me, there is no going back to trash."

I pull back from him, and he winks at me again. "Fuck me, please tell me there will be a gang bang because I'm hard as fuck right now," Abel jokes, and Armando shoots him a warning glare.

Abel holds his hands in the air. "Don't shoot me but tell me that you're not curious about what she would look like full of cocks, so damn full that when she is fucked to within an inch of her life that she leaks cum and looks so fucking beautiful."

"Who looks beautiful?" Romeo asks. Alex flanks his side and takes me in. It's not very often that his armor drops, and I'm no idiot, if I wasn't his best friend's sister, he would have fucked me by now, but he wouldn't betray my brother. This isn't some cute romance book where I'm the main character who falls for my brother's best friend, and we secretly date, and the brother is pissed when he finds out but eventually gets it when he sees them together. Nope, my life is more, my brother would pull out his gun, press it to Alex's skull, and pull the trigger and have no remorse. There are lines we don't cross here because it's life and death. Bianchi men don't do forgiveness, they do loyalty.

CHAPTER FIFTEEN

Genie

Everyone who is anyone in the mafia scene is seated around the room, but something doesn't feel right. Salvatore doesn't gather people for no reason, and it makes me nervous.

"Ladies and Gentlemen, I know you're all wondering why we are here tonight, and it's just simply because I want to celebrate my beautiful daughter. As you all know, she is due to be wed and has asked me if she can pick her own groom."

Laughter echoes around the venue. Fucking pigs, laughing as if the thought of a woman picking her own husband is absurd. Jaz reaches over and grasps my leg under the table.

"So, I have decided to up the ante, because who wouldn't want to marry a Bianchi woman. I want any eligible bachelors to try and sweep my daughter off her feet. I hope you all like the entertainment. I have my best fighter Alistair on the schedule for the night, and anyone game enough to take him on to win a chance with my daughter."

I look over at Street Rat, and he shrugs; this is the first that he has heard of it. Once Salvatore finishes his speech, he comes down to our table.

"Papa, why did you do that?"

"Because any man with my daughter needs to prove himself. Alistair has proved he is strong enough to look after my baby girl."

Romeo joins his father and claps him on the shoulder. "We don't need no pussy little bitch walking amongst us, you need a real man."

Jazlyn knows there is no point arguing, what her father says is final. He rules the family, and there is nothing that she can do that will change his mind.

"Are you ready?" Salvatore asks Street Rat, and he nods.

"I was born ready, especially if your daughter is the prize, no man will beat me."

"That's what I like to hear," Salvatore says with a laugh that bellows out of him and echoes around us.

"Romeo will take you back so you can get ready."

Street Rat stands from his chair and walks away with Romeo. Some old guy that could be a knock off for Tony Soprano gains Salvatore's attention, and he walks away. Jaz sighs, and her shoulders drop. I open my mouth to say something, but Armando shocks me when he leans forward.

"Don't worry, Princess, I might be willing to compete with that fucker, but any other man wins tonight, and he will end up in a shallow grave."

I know he doesn't trust Alistair or Abel, and he is right

to feel that way. The guy is always so fucking perceptive, and he makes the picture-perfect husband for her. But Jazlyn deserves more than that, she deserves the world. I just hope that none of us get ourselves killed in the process because I for one like to live.

"What's your deal?" Boo asks Armando, leaning back in his chair, his arms across his chest.

"My deal?" Armando asks, "Is that I don't trust you or your friend, but I will humor my future wife, and you can compete for her affection. You might be fun and fuck her like she is a porn star, but friend, I was here first, and I will be here last because deep down she knows who I am and what a future with me would look like. I grew up with these men, learned from them and I know what it takes to come out on top. You just have to know how to play the game, and I'm afraid you and your friend have come in too late."

"I look forward to beating you," Boo says with a laugh.

"Can you all stop talking about me as if I'm not here? I don't want to be married full stop, I want to travel. I want to experience life, not be tied down to one man for the rest of my life. So act all cocky, Jaffa, and while you might know my family, you don't know me or what I like, and maybe if you even want the smallest chance to be with me, maybe start paying attention."

Jaz pushes herself back, and her chair scrapes across the floor before she stands and storms away.

"Have you heard the story of the turtle and the hare?" I ask, standing from my chair, Armando barely glances up at me. "I'm the turtle."

Boo snorts, and Armando looks up and narrows his eyes at me. "You're a glorified bullet proof vest, Salvatore would kill you before he let you near his daughter. So if I were you, I would fuck her as much as you can now before she ends up with a real man."

Boo smirks at me and shakes his head. "My man, if you knew what he could do with his dick, you would be following that girl now and groveling. Because if we are winning from sexual performance, he has it in the bag, those piercings are a gift from God."

I clap Boo on the shoulder. "Thanks."

I wink at him, and I get up to find Jazlyn. I can't afford to lose sight of her tonight.

Crossing the makeshift dance floor where men are setting up the cage, I don't see her anywhere, so I beeline straight for the woman's bathroom. Jaz isn't stupid enough to go far, not with a room for of predators.

Pushing through the door, a woman in her mid-fifties, who looks like she has had more Botox in her life than I have had meals, runs her eyes over me and smiles. I ignore her. "Jaz, are you in here?"

"No, go away."

I laugh and find the stall on the end and knock. "I'm not going anywhere, your father would have my head if I did."

"I will make sure to have it made into a cement ornament and mount you on my wall."

I chuckle through the door. "Open up, you know you have to be out there front and center."

She unlocks the door and steps out. Her lashes are wet from crying, but it doesn't take from her beauty.

"I feel like I should just marry Armando to stop all this madness. My father would be happy with that choice, and I know how to handle him. A few months isn't enough to pick someone new."

"A few months is plenty of time. I know you have a connection with Alistair and Abel, and I meant it when I said I want to put myself in the running. There are some things that you don't know about me yet, but I'm so close to being able to tell you."

"And what if I don't want to choose, what then?"

"Do you trust me?"

She blinks at me and cocks her head slightly. She is a Bianchi; she has been taught to not trust anyone, not even her own family.

"I don't trust anyone, you know that, and especially not when people keep lying to me. I know Alistair and Abel are Street Rat and Boo."

My mouth falls open. "You do?"

She nods. "I do, the day that you and I..." She waves her arm around.

I smirk, she is thinking about me eating out her beautiful cunt after Street Rat fucked her. "He asked me if I trusted him, but he said the exact same thing the first time we met."

"Does he know that you know?"

She shakes her head no. "I'm waiting to see if he tells me."

"Princess, you know he can't, your father would kill him. He is helping me right now with something, and I promise that we will tell you everything soon."

I take her hands in mine, and she gives them a squeeze. "I'm going to put my trust in you, Genie, but you need to give me something."

"My real name is Archer Gene Barber, and my mother used to date your father. If you tell anyone, I will be murdered. I have a plan."

Her mouth falls open. "You used them as bait to see if anyone is coming after your family still. You need to warn them."

She goes to move past me, and I grab her wrist and push her against the closed door. "They know, Princess, they wouldn't have gone into this blindly. Just give me a bit more time, and I promise you that I will talk to your father. Promise me that I can trust you," I ask, leaning my forehead against hers.

"I promise," she says.

She nods, and I sigh win relief. That could have gone either way, and I'm glad she is willing to trust me. I just hope that she keeps her promise, I need to find out who my family's real enemies were. No one is truly friends in this world, you have allies that could turn on you at any minute. But those who killed my family were sneaky; they didn't announce their beef, and they didn't showcase the slaughter like most would. No, they came in and eradicated every last person, and I'm grateful that I managed to stay alive.

We move from behind the door, and when I lead her out into the hall, a figure catches me eye as it darts out. I grab Jaz's hand and drag her along behind me, and we see Isaac slithering away. I bet that asshole is reporting back to Armando on how long we were in there. Motherfucker.

Boo is talking to Alissa, one of the mob wives. "Watch Jaz, I just have a fucking parrot to kill."

Boo raises a brow at me, but I don't have time to explain. I cut through the tables of wives chatting to each other and see him duck down another hall, one that leads out to the alley behind the building. He doesn't get very far down, and when he hears the click of the gun, he freezes.

"Turn the fuck around now and slowly."

He raises his hands in the air and turns around and laughs. "Well, it looks like I'm busted."

"Why are you spying on me?"

"Tut, tut, Genie, why would you think that I was spying on you? We all know it's not a secret Armando wants Jazlyn followed, and if I had a chance with a woman like that, I would be paranoid that she wouldn't pick me."

"Answer the fucking question, we both know you're not stupid."

"The game ends when the King falls, but not when a Pawn takes the Queen."

I scratch my head. "What the fuck does that even mean? You're a walking, talking contradiction."

He laughs at me. "It's a dog-eat-dog world, Archer, and some secrets we need to hold on to so we are one of the last men standing."

"So, you heard. What do you want? If I kill you now, Salvatore will not be happy."

"What do I want? Hmm, world peace is a bit cliché, maybe I want in on the chance to win the girl."

I bellow out a laugh from deep in my throat. "You don't want the girl, you don't even like that kind of woman. You should have tried harder with that one because you're not fooling anyone."

"It seems you also know secrets. Right now, I don't need anything, but when I do, I will come see you."

I nod and put my gun back in its holster behind my suit

jacket. Fuck, shit is getting out of hand, and I need to warn Street Rat and Boo that Armando is about to know exactly who they are and that will be the end of them. Armando is an ass kisser.

The room erupts in cheers, and I turn and leave Isaac in the hall, pushing my way through until I find Boo, Jaz, and, to my surprise, Armando all seated at the table closest to the cage.

"Everything okay?" Boo asks, and I nod. We can't talk about this here, and we will need to do it in private. Isaac won't talk to Armando here, he isn't stupid enough to piss anyone off in public.

Salvatore steps into the cage. "Let's see if we have anyone willing to take on Alistair. Come on, who wants to be first?"

"I do," a voice says from the back of the room. People crane their necks to get a good look, but I instantly know who it is and so does Jaz. Ivan Kozlov. I should have guessed the Russians would be the first to get into the cage.

Ivan gets to the cage and shrugs his jacket off, unbuttons his shirt, and folds it neatly, placing it on a table full of horny housewives who giggle at him. One even tries to run her hand over his abs. Jaz rolls her eyes, but she watches as he removes his shoes and then his dress pants, leaving him in his boxer briefs. I give the man props; he is fucking built and hot as fuck.

"You two might want to wipe your drool," Boo laughs, looking between Jaz and me.

"Hell would have to freeze over before I married a Kozlov. I have heard stories about how they treat their women."

Armando laughs. "It seems like I'm not looking so bad after all."

"Shut up, Jaffa, we both know that if I married you, one of us would be dead within the first year."

Armando smirks at her and shrugs. "It would be a hell of a year though."

A hush falls over the room when Ivan steps into the cage, the guy is massive in height and fucking muscle. I don't know how Street Rat is going to be able to come out on top of this one. Street Rat sizes him up and fucking laughs at him, the crazy fucker. Ivan rushes him, and from there on out, Street Rat dominates the cage. He fights dirty like he would on the streets, and luckily for him, there are no rules, except today no one dies. Salvatore would end up with more enemies than he could fight.

After a few rounds, Ivan taps out, and the ref holds up Street Rat's arm. I really hope the Bianchi family know what they are doing. Killing a man's pride could be enough to warrant a war, maybe not today, and maybe not tomorrow, but one day Romeo will take over for Salvatore and Ivan for his father, and then what? People can hold grudges for a long time.

CHAPTER SIXTEEN

Jaffa

The fights are well and truly over for the night, and we all settle in for an evening of decadent food and endless flowing wine and whiskey. I have to give it to Salvatore, he knows how to throw a party. Everyone is dressed in their finest suits and shiniest Italian leather shoes. The women all glimmer with their diamond encrusted jewelry and their over-the-top evening dresses. It's a night of nights where the who's who of the mob world are invited to showcase their desires to wed Jaz. I never thought Salvatore would invite rival families, but I know he is always one step ahead of the game and probably has planned this evening right down to the last detail. There is always a purpose to his actions, I just need to decipher what they are tonight. He has kept his cards close to him these last few weeks, not revealing his inner thoughts to me or anyone for that matter. I don't know what he's cooking up, but the unease in the pit of my stomach with all that is going on around us with these two new slimeballs has me on edge.

Alistair and Abel have disappeared out the back to get Alistair cleaned up with the big Russian in there with them. Hopefully they get into a pissing contest back there and end each other. It would mean three less fuckers in the running as suitors for the Bianchi princess.

I watch Jazlyn carefully from across our table, and I know she can feel my gaze on her skin, but she still sits and attempts to act all nonchalant and unknowing. I know the effect my new fake persona has on her. If only I'd known how easy it would be to lure her in with my Emmy-worthy acting skills, I would have played the nice guy months ago.

"Armando, you're wanted at the bar." Salvatore nods in my direction as all eyes at the table turn to land on me.

I don't know when he got the message or who delivered it, but I know I have to do as Salvatore says. I nod in response before I allow my gaze to sweep across the table and settle on Jazlyn. I shoot her a sultry smirk I know she can't resist before I push my chair back, stand, and button up my tuxedo jacket.

I pad across the room and zigzag between the tables that are packed with all the mobsters in our district. I waltz past the Russian's table and notice they are all relaxed and having a great time, drinking our whiskey and eating our food. They look as though they're a part of our world as they chat amongst themselves without a care in the world that they are potentially sitting ducks in a room full of Italian made men and their associates.

I arrive at the bar where the bartender slides me an already poured whiskey before he carries on with his tasks of serving others. I move to the far corner where the lighting is dim and the chance of being ambushed is less. I press my back against the wall and my side into the bar before I take a sip of the mellow whiskey. It tastes like heaven on my parched lips and glides down my throat coating it like honey. One of the simplest pleasures always brings the most comfort.

My gaze catches movement from the other side of the bar when I spot Isaac heading toward me. He shoots me a look of triumph before he schools his features and pulls out his phone, indication for me to do the same.

"My man, how's this shitshow going for you?" Isaac fakes small talk.

I sip my whiskey and eye him with confusion. He's usually less theatrical in his deliverance of information so I know something is up or he's worried he's being watched. "What can I say other than a waste of my fucking time."

Isaac indicates for the barman to bring him a drink, and we both stand in silence as the noise of the crowd drowns out our thoughts. I sense Isaac has something he needs to get off his chest, and this isn't the best place for it, so I grab out my phone and message him before I place my phone screen down on the bar.

"Who would have thought that degenerate that has weaseled his way into the family would beat the Russian's ass? I think you've got yourselves a little problem there." Isaac glances at his phone and replies.

My phone buzzes on the counter, but I ignore it for the time being, not wanting to look like I'm eager to read the message sent to me if anyone is watching us. "Did you manage to get any intel on our friends?" I decide on direct questioning that could refer to any of our business dealings.

"Not a fucking thing. These fuckers are smart in their

movements and the way they conduct business. They're too careful, but we'll get a handle on them somehow." Isaac plays along nicely, and his answers flow nicely.

This is why he's my right-hand man. He knows how to read a room and what I'm thinking without me needing to say anything out loud. I pick up my phone and unlock it before I click on the text from Isaac.

> Isaac: Alistair and Abel are Street Rat and Boo. And to top off your great night, Genie is Archer Gene Barber.

"Motherfucker!" I seethe through gritted teeth. I wish I'd taken this conversation outside so I could react accordingly. I stare at my phone screen as the rage and betrayal about bursts out of me. The tight grip I have on my phone threatens to break it.

"I nearly got a bullet between the eyes for this one. Genie spared me for some dumb reason." Isaac whistles through his pursed lips before he places his tumbler against his mouth and throws back his whiskey in one go.

"Those fuckers!" I click my phone screen off and place it back in my pants pocket. I cannot react in anyway in here. I need to play it cool even though I want to grab the fucking microphone and announce it over the loudspeaker that we have three traitors in the building.

"What do you want me to do, boss?" Isaac stands and scans the room, always on guard and ready for action.

"Nothing."

He looks at me incredulously. "Nothing?" he repeats.

"We can't do shit in here." I rub my temple as the threat of a headache looms. The tension in my neck and shoulders is worse than ever before, but I'm glad I have this little piece of information about our little friends. It means I have the upper hand and can puppeteer them as I please.

Those dumb fucks have played right into the cobra's den, and I plan on using them until the minute they take their last breath. As for Genie, I always knew that fucker wasn't who he said he was. He is always so closed off and focuses on his job, never revealing anything about himself, and now I know why. His family was gunned down in cold blood, and he's out for revenge. I just need to work out why he's attached himself to the Bianchi family so tightly. What the fuck is the connection?

"Thanks, Isaac. Your job for tonight is done. Be careful and watch your back. I have a feeling these two-faced fucks will have a target on your back. The less people who know their secret the better." I indicate for him to leave through the back of the kitchen as it would be safer.

He slinks past the bar area and through the two-way swinging doors like an alley cat who thieved the night's fish from the shop. He disappears as quickly as he appeared, and I return my sights to the table of liars. I make my way back slowly and try to come up with a game plan with this new information I have acquired.

I notice Street Rat and Boo are back after the fight with the Russian, but Genie is nowhere to be seen. The hairs on the back of my neck prickle, and I hope that Isaac got out before Genie got a hold of him. I take my seat and can't help the knowing grin that spreads across my face as I stare at the slimeballs across from me.

"What the fuck is up your ass, man?" Boo glances at me with confusion.

"All will be revealed. Secrets don't stay hidden for long when the subjects are careless." I offer and grab the tumbler of whiskey in front of me and hold it up in a salute. I can sense the watchful gaze of Jazlyn as I swirl the whiskey around. "To old friends and new. May they fall from grace harder than they rose." I take a sip of my whiskey as the guests at the table stare at me as though I've lost my mind.

CHAPTER SEVENTEEN

Boo

I hear the words as they come out of Genie's mouth. Armando knows who we are, and in all honesty, I really don't give a fuck. It's the tunnel vision that I get when Jazlyn walks into the room, I can't believe that he brought her here.

"So, you know?" Street Rat asks her, and she nods.

"I do."

Street Rat nods. "Look, I'm sorry that we lied, but people like us would never be welcome in your world, but it doesn't matter. Armando will tell your father, and he will kill us. So, I think that it's best that we go home. It's been fun seeing how the other side lives, but it's not for us. Marry Armando. Too many lives will be at risk if you don't."

"So that's it?!" she yells. "You're just going to walk away."

"You bet your ass I am, Princess. Your father won't kill you, but he will end us and not even blink."

"Are you sure that Isaac will tell Armando?" I ask, and

all three of them level me with a stare. "Okay, it was worth asking, but fuck, is running really the answer? What about our families, Street Rat? If they find us, and they will because Armando found you once before, who's going to keep them safe?"

"He what?" Jaz asks.

"He came to me and wanted me to find The Lamp because he couldn't find it on his own."

"That's it," Genie says. "We give him the location in exchange for his silence."

Jaz laughs. "You really think that he won't run straight to my father in exchange for knowing where my father's stupid fight club is? No, he will want more, and I know what I have to do."

Tears spring to her eyes. "For what it's worth, I liked spending time with you, all of you, but the only person that can save the bloodshed is me. I give you all my word that your families will be safe."

She doesn't wait for anyone to reply, she turns on her Louboutin's and starts to walk away. Genie grabs her arm and pulls her back toward his body.

"We can't let you give up your life for us, Princess. Armando will want you to marry him."

A lone tear slides down her face. "I know, but if I do this, he will backoff, and you can find who hurt your family. Street Rat and Boo can go home, and their families will be safe. There is no other way. I have made up my mind, and I order you to let me leave. You will watch me walk away, and you won't try to stop me."

Genie drops her hand, and she steps back, looking up at him. "In an ideal world, I would have loved to have spent time with all three of you and had fun. But let's face it, I'm not a normal girl, who has the luxury of doing what she wants. I have to do what my father expects of me, and there isn't anything I can do about it."

Street Rat is done, he storms from the room. I know he liked her, even if it is unlike him to form any attachment to a girl he has fucked. I have to admit that I'm also drawn to her, but I also like to fuck, and a situation that involves a handful of people would have worked well for me. Now I have experienced that, I know what I will be looking for in the future. From my internet search, poly relationships are a big thing now, and I'm excited to find one. I wish it was with Jaz and Genie, that man fucks like a god.

"I will drive you home," Genie tells her, and she nods. Jaz hesitantly walks up to me and places her hand on my cheek.

"Please make sure he is okay. I wish things were different, but I hope you understand it's the only way that I can save him and you. I think you're pretty special, Boo, I wish nothing but good things for you."

"Back at you, Princess. If you ever need to escape for a few days, or you just need multiple orgasms, you know where to find us."

She giggles and leans in to press her lips against mine before pulling back. "Take care of yourself."

I nod, and Genie takes her hand and leads her from his house. I watch them through the large bay glass windows until the Range Rover pulls out onto the road.

"Are they gone?" Street Rat asks from behind me. I turn to face him, and he is no longer dressed like he belongs in the mafia, he is back in his street gear, looking like his regular self.

"They are, let's get out of here. There has to be a party back home with our name on it."

That makes him smile at me. I know he doesn't really want to leave, he will want to storm in guns blazing, except he hates guns, and you really can't take a knife to a gun fight when the mafia are involved.

We didn't have much shit when we came here so it makes it a hell of a lot easier to leave. I called Siska to pick us up, and not long after, she pulls into the driveway in my beat-up piece of shit. I'm going to miss the life of luxury; a guy could have gotten used to that.

Street Rat jumps into the back seat, and Siska doesn't even look at him. I know that she is still heartbroken, but he isn't the guy for her. I used to think that she needed to meet a rich man, and being on the inside of that world, I hope she meets someone normal, and they live in the suburbs with a white picket fence and have a perfect and happy life.

"Oh shit, you were staying here and didn't invite me?"

"Baby sis, this world isn't for the likes of us. The men around here don't deserve you, and there is no way in hell I would have allowed them to meet you. Fuck, I would have preferred you and Street Rat to get together."

"Don't be a dick," Street Rat says, irritation lacing his tone.

"Shit, I'm sorry, Sis, I didn't mean to be insensitive."

Siska shrugs and reverses down the driveway.

"It's fine, I actually met someone while you were away. He will be at the party tonight."

Street Rats eyes meet mine in the rear-view mirror, and

I smirk. We are on the same wavelength, that poor bastard is going to wish he never met my sister by the end of the night. Or he will be strong enough to date her if he can handle us.

"What's that look? I swear to God, if you ruin this for me, I will kill you myself. It's not even anything serious. We are just having fun, and I don't plan on having a serious relationship here. I plan to wait until college and find a nice boy. But every girl deserves a bad boy just once."

I put my fingers in my ears to block out her talking. "Lalala, I don't want to hear it."

The drive back to Kingston Village doesn't take that long. Siska blasts the radio, puts on Eminem, and we rap the entire way home while Street Rat has his headphones on and stares at his phone.

Siska parks in my usual spot, and Street Rat jumps out the second the car stops and runs over to his mom's house. She is out the front tending to her garden, which is normally where she is when she isn't at work. He picks her up and wraps his arms around her and spins her around, making her laugh.

"Hey, Lalah," I call from our side of the yard as Street Rat places her on her feet.

"Hey, Boo boo. It's good to have you boys back. We missed you around here."

"We missed you too."

I wave and head inside. My father won't be home; he never is, and it's fine. Both Siska and I are grown now, we don't need him hovering around.

Street Rat comes back over not long after dinner as all our friends start to arrive. It slightly pisses me off that they planned this party here at my house, and I wasn't even supposed to be here, but I don't dwell on it for too long. Someone hands me a red solo cup on my way outside.

"Boo, my man," Sweet Cheeks says, pulling me in for a hug. "Thought you had ditched us for good."

I pull back. "It seems like you made yourselves at home while I was gone."

"Nah, it's not like that, we were looking out for Sissy. She told Big Daddy that the parties would still be on, and we came to keep an eye on her. Sparky punched some preppy dude in the face for feeling her up."

"Thanks for looking out, man, I appreciate it, but we are back now."

We do another man shake, and I head over to the fire pit. Street Rat jumps his back fence and joins me. The sour look on his face tells me that he is itching for a fight tonight, which won't end well for some poor fucker.

Bringing the red solo cup to my mouth, I see Siska sneak around the side of the house in a very tight dress. Motherfucker, that girl was so sweet and innocent. I worry that hanging out with this crowd while I was gone has corrupted her. Over my dead body will I let any fucker ruin her future. Girls from around here never leave, they get knocked up in high school and never leave. If you go to the local strip club, half those bitches I went to high school with, and their baby daddies are useless as fuck, so they have to strip to make ends meet. I love a good strip show as much as the next man, but it irks me that these dicks don't step up.

"What the fuck?" Street Rat yells abruptly, standing up and moving across the lawn before I can even register what is happening. I throw my cup to the ground and follow after him, I need to protect whatever poor fuck he is about to murder.

I freeze momentarily when I see he has Isaac pinned by his throat to the brick wall behind the house. Siska screams, and I race to her side.

"Help him, Boo. Please, Street Rat will kill him."

I snort, that slimy motherfucker. "Sis, you need to go inside."

"No!"

"Why the fuck are you here?"

I watch and wait for Isaac to reply.

"I don't know what you mean, I'm here to see Siska."

I turn my gaze to my sister. "You told him your name? Fuck, you know better."

"Don't fucking play stupid with me, Isaac. Why the fuck are you here? Where is Armando?"

"Who is Armando?" Siska asks.

"Fuck, Sweet Cheeks," I yell, and he comes to my aid, taking Siska and throwing her over his shoulder.

Isaac laughs at Street Rat. "How do you think I found information about you both? Your sister loves to talk. I have been told to watch you. Now I suggest that you let me go, because if I don't check in, Armando would be forced to tell Salvatore about you and where you are."

That stumps Street Rat, Armando hasn't squealed yet. My stomach churns at the thought of Jaz agreeing to marry the guy.

"Or maybe I will go straight to Salvatore myself."

"Fuck," Street Rat yells, letting go of Isaac, and punches the wall, letting out a hiss of pain.

"Go to Salvatore, I dare you," I say, moving closer. "Because while that might get us killed, we have a chance that Jazlyn would get us spared, but you, something tells me that if we killed you, Salvatore would just have you replaced, and Armando would have no say in the matter. Isn't that how it works in the mafia, everyone is expendable?"

"How about we call a truce? Let me talk with Siska; she made it clear that she wasn't looking for anything serious and neither am I. I'm not stupid enough to drag a nice girl like her into my lifestyle. And for the record, Armando has no idea that I'm even here tonight, he is with Jazlyn."

"Fuck," Street Rat growls, shaking his hand. "I think I broke something."

I take a deep breath in. "Fine, go and talk to my sister, but you hurt her, and I will kill you myself."

He nods and pushes off the wall, and Street Rat shoulder checks him on his way past. I turn and nod at Sweet Cheeks, and he lets Siska go. Fuck me, this is getting way to complicated now.

"Let's go ice your hand. Why the fuck would you punch a brick wall for, anyway? You should have aimed for his face."

He laughs at me, and after we walk inside of the house, I get a tea towel and some ice and hand it to him.

"This is fucked up. We are going to need to talk to Jaz and see if Armando is going to keep quiet. We can't afford to bring mafia problems here. I won't risk Mom and Siska, and why the fuck would you let that weasel talk to your sister?"

"Because as much as it pains me to let him talk to her, we can't have him running back to anyone and tell them our whereabouts. Salvatore isn't going to be happy that you just up and left. I will call Genie and see what he knows."

His eyes look into mine, he has always had a knack of knowing what I'm thinking. "You like him."

I shrug. "Maybe, he fucked like a damn God. Would I have jumped at the chance to be in some weird four-way fuck fest with him, Jaz, and us? Of course because that kind of fucking is fire. Will I pine around after him? I doubt it. What about you?"

He leans back against the counter and looks down at the floor. "Fucks me, man. I felt something between us that first night, and all of this happening has reminded me of why I never wanted to get close to anyone. It fucking hurts to walk away."

I nod because I get it, we don't get close to anyone, especially not a lover because heartbreak fucking sucks, and we usually don't want to drag anyone into this life. Who would want to love on this side of town, where most people live below the poverty line. But above all else, family comes first, and relationships can blur those lines. That isn't something either of us would give up without a fight.

CHAPTER EIGHTEEN

Jazlyn

I waltz into Armando's office without knocking, a little extra sway in my hips. He is on the phone behind his desk, and I flop down onto the expensive Italian leather couch. His eyes meet mine, and he follows my movements. He knows why I am here. He isn't stupid.

"Just get it done," he snaps and ends the call, pushing himself up from his chair. He moves around the desk and sits on the couch opposite me, and as he leans back, his legs fall open.

"I wasn't expecting you," he says with a smirk.

"Cut the shit, Jaffa, I know that you know."

"That I know what? That you fucked two street mutts or that they somehow managed to con their way into your life and pretend to be wealthy?"

"What's it going to cost me for you to not tell my father? They have gone now. I will marry you if that's what it takes."

He rubs his chin. "We both know that you would have

married me anyway, no one else is worthy of being in your family. Now strip."

"What?"

"I didn't stutter, Princess, stand up and strip down to your underwear."

I cut an icy glare his way, and his eyes dance with amusement. Standing, I don't break eye contact, I untuck my silk blouse from my pencil skirt and undo the buttons one by one until there are none left, and I let the material fall from my shoulders. Next, I reach behind and undo the zip, shimmying the skirt down my tanned legs until it falls to the floor, and I step out of it.

Jaffa sucks his bottom lip into his mouth and lust fills the air; it's so damn thick even I can feel it.

"On your hands and knees and crawl to me."

He moves the coffee table between us with his foot as I get onto all fours, and I crawl toward him. When I reach his legs, I push up onto my knees and wait for what he has in store for me next.

"Unbuckle my belt and pull out my cock."

Shock covers his face when I reach forward, unclip his belt, and undo his slacks, pulling the zipper down slowly. I have always been curious what Jaffa is packing, he gives off this big dick energy, like he is overcompensating for something.

His cock is hard, and when I slide down his boxer briefs, my mouth falls open, making him chuckle. "There is no way that is going to fit."

My sudden discomfort makes him laugh even harder. "Baby girl," he says, leaning forward, cupping my chin as his thumb swipes across my bottom lip, no doubt smudging the red lipstick.

"It will fit, now be a good girl and climb onto my lap."

Doing as he asks, I straddle his lap, and his hands fall to my waist. "I'm going to fuck you, Jazlyn, on every fucking surface of this office, and then you will tell your father tonight that you have made your choice, and out of respect for me, you sent the street scum packing. Do you understand?"

I nod, trying to will the fucking tears away. I don't know why I'm so upset. I loved fucking them, but it never could have worked. It just tears my heart out knowing I will never see them again, and that Genie has to watch me with Armando. We can't do anything about the feelings we have for each other.

Armando stands, his hands clapped to my ass as he takes me with him. He sets me down on his desk, and I lean back on my arms and watch as he unbuttons his shirt and shrugs it off. I have never seen him without a shirt on before, and my eyes don't know where to look first. The impeccably toned abs, or the V that screams look at my cock, or the tattoos that line his skin. His right peck draws me in, the flowers are Jasmines, I know because I have them planted everywhere in the yard. As a small child, I wanted to be called Jasmine and made everyone call me that for two years. I hated that I couldn't find my name on anything. I was obsessed.

I reach out and run my nail over it, the old clock has no hands. "Why is the clock blank?"

"Because it will read the time that we are married."

My mouth falls open, and he leans down and covers my

mouth with his. Kissing him is a power play, one where we both fight for dominance. He wins in the end when he rips my thong off in one swift movement, leaving me bare, and his large cock presses against my core. The greedy bitch begs for him to push a little harder, but he doesn't; he just leaves the tip almost about to breach my hole, and he trails kisses along my neck and down to my lace bra. He moves the material aside and covers my nipple with his mouth, sucking until they are hard. A moan escapes me, and I don't try and hide it, I buck my hips, and his cock pushes harder against me. He is way too thick to just slip in.

His large hand presses against my chest, and he forces me back. I lay back and lean on my elbows so I can watch. He wraps his hand around his length and runs it up and down my slit few times until he lines us up and thrusts hard inside me. I scream at the intrusion, I'm stretched as much as my body can take. He slowly pulls back, and I watch as he watches his cock slide out of me.

"Fuck," he growls. "Your cunt looks good taking my cock. I can't wait to call you mine and fuck you any time I please. I have waited a long time for this."

He thrusts into me again, and as my body finally eases, pleasure takes over. He pulls my body up to his, and I wrap my arms around his neck. He moves us away from the table and walks us close to the large sliding doors that overlook the city, and he presses my back against the glass, brushing my hair from my face. I grind against him needing the friction as our lips meet, and it's like something has changed, its soft and full of unspoken meanings. We don't hate each other, not really, it's always been a game of cat and mouse. His measured thrusts, and his tongue moving against mine washes away the tension in my body and replaces it with the low build of an orgasm.

Jaffa opens the sliding door and walks us through it before lifting me off his cock and making me slide down his body. A small whimper slips past my lips at the loss between my thighs and how empty I feel.

"Turn around and put your hands on the railing and spread your legs. I want you to scream my name when you come so the whole city knows who you belong to."

I quickly do as he asks, needing him to fill the void he has just left. With my hands on the railing, he kicks my legs apart further and steps up behind me. He wastes no time burying himself deep inside me; he starts to thrust fast, and the friction has my body ready to explode. He reaches around and his finger finds my clit, and his thrusts become short and sharp until my pussy clamps down around his dick, and I scream his name for the entire city to hear. He must come with me, because his chest presses against my back.

"You made the right decision," he whispers against my skin.

"I really hope so, because the second they are no longer safe, I walk. I don't care if we are married. I will have you killed alongside them, even if I have to pull the trigger myself."

Armando might think he is in control, but he isn't. My father is, and even Romeo has more pull. A few shed tears from my eyes, and my brother will get trigger happy.

"You really feel that deeply about them?" he asks, taking a step back, and his flaccid cock slides out of me easily. I turn to face him and shrug.

"Maybe, it was still new, but they don't deserve to die. All they wanted to do was get close to me and get to know me."

I have never seen Jaffa be vulnerable, and its uncharted territory for me. Pissed Jaffa, asshole Jaffa, that man I know how to deal with. But this one, not so much. He reaches out and takes my hand.

"And you enjoyed being with them all…at the same time?"

I nod, I won't lie to him. "It was exhilarating, having them all worshiping me. If roles were reversed, and it was Romeo and he had multiple women, no one would blink an eye. I just want to live, and with them, I wasn't Jazlyn Bianchi. I was just Princess, a girl who wanted to have fun, and her Papa wasn't mafia, and she didn't have to marry anyone she didn't want to. I got to feel free."

Armando nods. "Let's get you inside and cleaned up."

He leads me inside and pulls out a box of tissues and cleans his cum from between my legs before I get dressed.

"We are going to see your father, he is downtown meeting with your uncle, Tiny."

I nod, Tiny isn't my blood uncle, but he has been part of my life for as long as I can remember. He owns a small Italian restaurant which I'm sure is one of the many businesses my father launders money through.

Once Armando has finished putting himself back together and is nothing short of perfect, we head downstairs, and we both slide into his red Ferrari.

We drive in silence, and it's not an uncomfortable silence, just slightly tense due to my nerves. I don't even know why I'm nervous to tell my father, I'm sure that he will be delighted that I am going with his choice. Maybe it will be the underlying 'I told you so' that he won't vocalize.

We pull into the parking lot of Tiny Italian. The name is hilarious because Tiny is not small by any stretch of the imagination, he is well over six foot tall and a tank.

We both slide out of the Ferrari, and Armando links our hands. Guess this is something that I better get used to. We walk hand in hand across the parking lot, and Jaffa pulls the door open, and it chimes as we walk in. My father, Romeo, and Alex are all talking to Tiny until they pause and look our way.

"Nipote, it's so nice to see you again. It's been too long."

I drop Armando's hand and walk into Tiny's embrace. He wraps his arms around me and squeezes me to his chest.

I laugh as he also suffocates me. "It's only been a few weeks, Uncle."

He pulls back and looks at me. "A few weeks too long and look how thin you are," he tsks. "Why don't you all take a seat, and I will bring out some food, since clearly none of you men are feeding the girl."

My father leads us to a table in a private room, and we all take a seat. "Armando said that you needed to talk to me, is everything okay?"

I nod. "It is, I have made my choice, and I am going to marry Armando. It's time that I do what's best for this family."

"I see," is all my father says.

I swallow that hard lump in my throat. "And you will need to find a new fighter, I sent Alistair away."

My father clears his throat. "And why would you do that without asking me first?"

My eyes scan the men at the table, and I sit up straighter in my chair. "Because I'm Jazlyn Bianchi, and I don't need a reason, just like you and Romeo don't. It's about time that you both stopped treating me like a little girl."

"Is that so?"

I nod, and he studies me. "Then it's decided, your brother and I have business to take care of tonight, and if you can handle yourself then you can go unpunished for screwing and running off my prized fighter. If not, then you better hope that you can find him and convince him to come back."

I nod again, and Armando squeezes my leg. "I guess we have a wedding to plan," my brother says, breaking the tension, and I sigh in relief that it's over. I have no doubt in my mind that whatever business they have to take care of, I'm not going to like one bit, but I have no choice if it means saving those I care about.

CHAPTER NINETEEN

Genie

Fuck, I can't let Jazlyn marry Armando just to keep my secret. It's time that I manned up and went to Salvatore. I wanted justice for myself, to earn it on my own merits, but not at the expense of other people.

I make my way down the hall to the Salvatore's office and knock.

"Come in," he bellows, his voice echoing from beyond the door. I open it to find he is on the phone, and he holds a finger up, stopping me from opening my mouth.

"Get it done, Romeo, your sister wants to believe that she is ready so I trust you will take care of her."

He ends the call and looks up at me. "What can I do for you?"

"Can I have your word that you will hear me out before you blow my brain out?"

Salvatore narrows his eyes at me, "I give you my word."

I sigh in relief, but I don't relax since he still might very well put a bullet between my eyes. "I can't let Jazlyn go through with marrying Armando."

He eyes me warily but lets me continue talking. "She is doing it so Armando won't squeal, but I need to rewind my story for it to all make sense to you. My mother was Alissa Barber, and the night she died, she stuffed me into her suitcase and told me not to come out until she came back to get me. As you know, no one in my family survived that night except me. I knew where the burner phones were, and I was taught to call a number if anything bad ever happened."

Salvatore nods and listens. "I grew up needing answers¾wanting revenge¾and I knew the enemy I was up against would be too big for me to just walk in and throw my name around. I didn't want to lie to get this job, but it was my only in with this world. I don't suspect you, so this wasn't some scheme to ruin you. I always had a gut feeling it was the Russians. Well, you know the family history, and I'm afraid now that Ivan was shamed, that they will retaliate. I never wanted Jaz in harm's way, but that girl has a way of getting herself involved."

We sit in silence for a few minutes, my stomach in knots. "And how does Armando fit into all of this?"

"He doesn't really, he just knows that Alister and Abel are not really who they say they are. I needed to try and draw out my enemies."

I lean forward and slide a letter across his desk. "I found this in my mother's belongings. It's addressed to you."

He picks up the envelope and opens it, pulling out a letter. I wait for him to read it, and if I'm not mistaking, a lone tear wells in his eye.

"You have really put me in a hard position, kid, so let's

keep this between ourselves for now. Your mother was the love of my life, and it killed me when we couldn't be together. I had to marry an Italian girl from a family my father approved of, and fuck... I have done the exact same thing to my own children."

Salvatore's phone vibrates on the desk, he picks it up and bellows down the line. I can hear gunshots from where I'm standing, and my heart rate accelerates.

"You better find my fucking daughter or not show your face around here again."

Salvatore squeezes his phone and looks at me. "Gather everyone, we have someone who thinks they can take my child from me."

I nod and send out an SOS, so everyone will meet outside within fifteen minutes. "Do we have any information to go off?"

Salvatore fills me in on their meeting with the Russians, and I'm still convinced they are behind my family's demise, but right now, we need to get Jaz back.

"Who knew that she was going on a run tonight?"

"Myself, Romeo, Alex, Tiny, and Armando."

I pull my keys from my pocket. "Let's go talk to Tiny."

"Are you insinuating that he has something to do with this?" Salvatore asks, falling in step with me.

"Are you insinuating it was your son and his best friend or Armando. We need to make sure that Tiny didn't tell anyone."

I dial Armando. "What?" he snaps. "I'm busy."

"Too busy to help find your fiancée? She has been taken."

"From where? By whom?"

"We don't know, we are going to talk to Tiny. I suggest you talk to Isaac and make sure he has kept his mouth fucking closed because we will be paying him a visit next."

I end the call and slip into the driver's side of my Range Rover. Salvatore gets into the passenger side, and I don't waste any time reversing out of the garage and flooring it all the way to the other side of town. Armando's red Ferrari is already parked. Both Salvatore and I exit the car and stalk inside, where Armando and Isaac are both standing side by side. Everyone that works here is huddled into some booths, and Armando has his gun firmly in his grip.

Salvatore walks over to Armando and claps him on his shoulder. "Put your weapon away. Tiny is a family friend, and we do not disrespect family."

Armando reluctantly reholsters his weapon. "I never breathed a word to anyone, I swear," Tiny says.

"I don't doubt you, but this is my only daughter, and the only place we spoke about her whereabouts was here, so we have to look into your staff."

One man in particular, who looks to be in his early twenties, is sweating profusely, and his hands are trembling.

"Him," I say, pointing at the man.

"W...what? I don't know anything."

"Salvatore, are you okay to wait here while we take him into the kitchen to question him?"

Salvatore nods, and Isaac grabs the man by his shirt and rips him from his chair.

Armando, Isaac, and I walk into the kitchen, and Isaac throws the guy against a stainless-steel work bench.

"Start talking. We know you know something.

Everyone else was nervous because there was a gun, but you were squirrelly, and in my experience, only rats get nervous like that," I say.

Isaac pulls out a knife from the block and steps forward. "You need to talk or I'm going to gut you. I was balls deep in pussy, and I'm starting to get blue balls. When that happens, I'm not generally a nice person."

His shoulders slump, and you can see him give in to the fact that he is going to die here today. "I don't know his name, but some gang banger paid me three hundred bucks to plant a device. I needed the money, my mom is sick."

Isaac doesn't wait for him to explain further, he drives the knife into the man's stomach, and he slumps against Isaac's body.

I don't wait for him to finish the job; I go into the back room where all types of men meet. I scour the room and find the fucking listening device under the table, and I take it back to Salvatore. Romeo and Alex have joined us now, which makes the tension in the room almost unbearable. Armando and Isaac walk from the kitchen, Isaac has blood on his clothes and still grips the knife in his hand.

"You will need to clean that mess up," Isaac says to Tiny. He nods. Armando flies across the room and gets in Romeo's face.

"You better step down," Romeo warns.

"You should have been looking after your sister. This world is no place for a woman, especially not my fucking woman."

Huh, I never actually thought Armando really cared about Jaz. I always figured that she was a means to an end for him, but his reaction to her being missing tells me otherwise.

Romeo scoffs, "Your woman? Give me a break, she was boning him and those other assholes just last week."

Salvatore cuts me a glare, and I shrug, now isn't the time to get into it with my boss.

My phone vibrates, and Boo's name pops up on the screen. I send him to voicemail, now also isn't the time to organize a booty call.

Isaac hands the knife to Tiny. "Can I rely on you to make this vanish?"

Tiny nods.

Isaac's phone belts out the apple ringtone, breaking the silence we lapsed into. He slides it from his pocket, and his brows furrow. "Butterfly, what's wrong?"

He listens, and he nods as whoever this butterfly is talks, then he hands the phone to me.

"Hello?"

"Fuck, please tell me what I'm seeing is a huge fucking joke," Street Rat shouts down the line.

"That depends on what you're seeing," I say.

"Check your fucking phone," Boo yells in the background. I hold Isaac's phone to my ear and pull mine out of my pocket. I open it, and my heart plummets into my stomach. It's a photo of Jazlyn tied up.

I put the phone down on the table, and Salvatore and the others all look at it.

"It's true, where can we meet?"

"The corner of South and East street. The building there belongs to a friend, and it won't look suspicious having the mafia turn up."

I end the call and hand Isaac back his phone. "We need to go, the people who took Jazlyn are after the Barbers."

We leave Tiny to clean up the mess and all file out and split into our own cars. Jaz better be okay, or heads are going to roll, and a war will break out. You don't take the mafia boss's daughter and get away with it. Innocent lives will be lost until she is back in the safety of her home.

The tires screech on the road as I take the last corner and hurtle toward where Street Rat said to meet. The blood in my veins courses through me and singes my insides as my rage roars in my pounding head. Whomever the fuck has taken my Jazlyn is going to fucking pay in the most depraved way. I can't wait to get my hands on them and gut them like a fish, remove their innards, and deliver them to their loved ones.

I've barely parked the car when I spot Boo and Street Rat to the side of the building. They've come on their own. Smart guys. They know as well as I do that only the best of the best will retrieve her without getting killed. I storm toward them, and their looks of rage mirror mine.

"What the fuck happened?" Street Rat eyes me accusingly, and I don't fucking blame him. It's my duty to protect her and keep her out of harm's way. It's my fucking job to ensure she's safe, and I failed.

I pace in front of them as I come up with a game plan. "I don't fucking know. I don't fucking know how the hell they got her." I groan as a pain I never thought I'd ever feel digs into my chest and almost suffocates me.

Armando arrives in his sleek red Ferrari, and as he climbs out, I can see he too is genuinely worried. "Romeo and Salvatore have gathered their men and are meeting at their usual place," he announces as he stalks toward us and stops a few feet away.

His cautious gaze travels over the three of us and settles back on me. I can see his accusations flying at me without even uttering a word.

"Spit it out!" Street Rat glares at him.

"I see the vermin and their master are once again called to help." Armando places his cigarette in his mouth and lights it. The red glow of the tip is the only light amongst the darkness.

"Fuck you." Boo flips him the finger and grants him a lopsided, goofy grin. Always the clown.

Armando looks at him, and a sly smirk quirks the corner of his mouth. "You'd like that, wouldn't you?" He winks condescendingly.

"I'd fuck you until the only name that would fall from your lips was mine." Boo steps forward and grabs the cigarette out of Armando's fingers and drags in a lungful of tobacco before handing it back.

"Well, boys, now that we have that over and done with, let's get to business. Yes, we know you know who we are and all that shit, but that's not important right now. We need to find Jaz." I rub the back of my neck as the thought of someone hurting her circles though my brain.

The obnoxious sound of an ice cream truck screams into the silence, and I realize it's Street Rat's phone. He slides it out of his pocket and stares at it before he glances at Boo and answers it.

"Yo, who's this?" Street Rat's gaze connects with mine, and I know it's the fucking kidnappers.

My insides turn to molten lava, and I'm about to

explode with anger as I watch helplessly as Street Rat nods in response to their talking.

"I need video proof or no dice." Street Rat ends the call.

"What the fuck, dude?!" Boo pushes at Street Rat's shoulder.

"I'm waiting for evidence that she's still alive. I had to play it cool, like we don't give a fuck about her." He trains his eyes on his phone screen.

"What did they want in return?" Armando steps closer to get a better look at the phone screen.

"They want your head on a platter." Street Rat glances up at me and gives me a look.

I know he'd deliver my head no matter what if it meant saving her. "They can have me. I'm going in alone."

"Hold your fucking horses there for a God damn minute, sex on legs." Boo grips my muscled bicep in his large hand, his fingers digging into my flesh. "I'm not ready to give up your hot piece of ass. We can do this as a team. A fucked-up team of misfits, but a team none the less. Right, Street Rat?"

"Here." Street Rat holds his phone out in the middle of us and presses on the video message.

My gut twists as the sight of her, all bruised and blood-ied. The ropes that bind her dig into her delicate flesh, and the purple bruises that decorate her skin send a rage through me like a tornado. She glares at the phone screen with a look of defiance, and I know she will survive this.

"Fuck," Armando grits through clenched teeth.

"That graffiti is in Ajax territory," Boo says as he takes the phone from Street Rat and replays the clip.

I can't fucking watch it again so I look up at the starless

sky and come to terms this may be the last time I ever see the world like this.

"Fucking slimy cunts. They're not far. Let's go." Street Rat taps Boo on the shoulder and grabs his phone back.

"The who territory?" Armando asks the question I suddenly can't.

"They're a rival street crew from Kingston Village. This won't take long. We'll be in and out in a matter of minutes." Street Rat is all business, like he has had a show down to this magnitude before.

"You'll get yourselves killed. I can't have that on my shoulders. I know they want me, and I'll hand myself over. There's no need for all this bloodshed tonight, boys." I try to convince them, but I know it's pointless.

"No fucking way we're missing out on this carnage." Boo grabs me behind the head and pulls my mouth into his. "I'm protecting your dick at all costs, and I think Jaz will thank me for it, hopefully in depraved ways." He winks before he slaps me on the ass and follows Street Rat to their car.

"Follow at a safe distance. We don't want them knowing we're coming in at once," Street Rat calls as he slams his door.

Armando and I climb into my car as it's less noticeable than his Ferrari. I ease out onto the road and follow Street Rat and Boo a few car lengths behind. The buildings as we travel through this part of town become more damaged and every second one is boarded up. Where the fuck did they take our girl? Street Rat pulls up in front of a dilapidated building that looks like it has been sprayed with bullet holes. The windows are boarded up, and the main entry is blocked with rusted steel bars. I don't know who the fuck these guys are, but I'm about to find out.

"Stay in the car. She doesn't need all of us dead." I shoot Armando a warning look before I reach down and grab my Glock from under my seat. I climb out of my car, say my prayers, and grip my Glock as though my life depends on it.

I slink across the road, the cover of darkness on my side, and manage to conceal myself down the side of the building next to a side door without causing a stir. I scan the area and spot a familiar looking car. "Fuck!" I hiss through clenched teeth to no one in particular. Romeo's distinctive car sits down the road in the open for all to see.

"What the fuck are you doing?" Street Rat slinks in beside me with Boo right behind him.

"Getting shit done. I'm going in alone. You two stay out here."

"I don't fucking think so." Street Rat argues. His need to save his princess overshadows his death wish.

"Romeo is in there somewhere. This bullshit is my fault. If they want me, they got me." I glare at Boo and Street Rat and hope to all fuck they stay out of it. Before they can argue with me, I kick the door down and ready my gun as I step through into the dusty and dank darkness.

The thump of my blood punching through my veins echoes in my head, the steady beat calming my nerves. I was trained for this, and I would sacrifice myself to save her. I slink through the room and head to a set of stairs, taking them two at a time until I reach the landing. It is eerily quiet in here, and a sense of doom settles in my chest.

"Jesus, slow the fuck down," Boo whispers as he sidles

up beside me with Street Rat on the other side. "What's the plan, boss?"

"Get out of here," I whisper at them, annoyed they're about to get their heads blown off once we storm into the room.

"Boo, you got left, I'll take the right, and Genie, take the center. On three. One. Two. Three." Street Rat shouts as he kicks the door off its hinges.

In synchronized movements, we storm the room, guns blaring, bullets flying everywhere. We have the rival gang members dead in a few seconds flat that my brain barely catches up with my movements. Smoky dust floats in the air, highlighted by the dim light of the streetlamp outside. Distinct metallic tang coats the air as the dead fuckers bleed out on the floor.

"Well, that was fun." Boo fist-bumps Street Rat before he goes in search of anyone still alive. "Guys!" Boo shouts from a room that's connected to this one.

Street Rat jumps over a dead body as he heads toward Boo. "Fucking hell." I catch up to them and stop in my tracks when my gaze lands on the bodies in the center of the room.

Romeo and Salvatore are tied together with their throats slit. I race to their side, my heart in my throat. I check for a pulse, but there is nothing. "Fuck!" I roar. Jaz won't survive this. A groan catches my ear, and I turn to see Alex lying in a pool of blood. I squat down beside him, putting myself in his eyeline.

"Why didn't you wait for us?" I snap at him. I don't bother asking how the fuck they knew she was here. They were supposed to gather their men and wait.

"We didn't think so low scum would have the manpower to beat us. Save her, she is all the Bianchi family have left. Make her strong. Please put me out of my misery."

He lifts his shirt, and I grimace, seeing that the fuckers gutted him. It's a surprise that he is still alive. Without so much as a word, I aim my Glock at him, ready to give him what he wants. He closes his eyes and starts to pray. I wait for him to finish and pull the trigger.

I can't think at that point, all I can see is white hot rage as I tear through the rooms in the building searching for her. My eyes burn like acid as the need to find her alive consumes me. I kick down a door at the far end of the hall and spot her laying on her side.

I study her, unable to move my legs when I see the small rise and fall of her ribcage, and my world crashes into me. I step forward and scoop her up into my arms, cradling her against me. "It's okay. I'm here," I whisper as I carry her toward the other two.

"Jaz," Street Rat's voice cracks as he takes in her bruised and bloodied figure.

"I'm taking her to the hospital. Can you deal with everything else?" My pleading eyes regard the two men I'm about to leave in charge to take care of the only family I have known. I trust them to be respectful of Salvatore's and Romeo's bodies. "I'll have my men here to help."

"We'll clean up." Boo watches Jaz carefully, his hand extended, wanting to touch her but too afraid she may break.

I leave the dead bodies behind as I carefully carry Jaz

down the stairs when I come face to face with Armando. His breaths are shallow as he clutches his stomach.

"Is she okay?" His wild eyes rake over her looking for signs of life.

"She'll be okay. What the fuck happened to you?" I look him up and down and notice the seeping blood as it soaks his suit shirt and pants.

"More of the fuckers arrived, but I killed them. They're around the side of the building," he groans as he hunches forward.

"Fuck, Armando, get in the car with me. I'm taking you both to the hospital, call your doctor to meet us there." I grip Jaz in one arm and try to support Armando to the car as I leave behind the piles of dead bodies thanks to my last name.

I don't know how Jaz is ever going to forgive me. This secret wasn't supposed to kill anyone. My family suffered enough. I hope they find the fuckers I need and keep them alive so I can get my retribution.

Isaac runs out, covered in blood. "Fuck, are you good?"

I nod just as a shot pops off in the building, and he looks at me. "Go, I want the leader alive. I have some questions for him."

Isaac eyes the three of us, then nods before he runs off into the building.

CHAPTER TWENTY

Street Rat

I watch as the bodies of Salvatore, Romeo, and Alex are placed in body bags and loaded into a white van. Boo steps up beside me and places a hand on my shoulder.

"How the fuck do you tell someone their family just died?"

I feel Boo shrug. "I have no idea."

"Let me go, you piece of fucking shit," Ajax spits. I turn to face the man that Isaac dragged out into the open.

"I found a rat, and I have been told to keep him alive, but fuck, it's hard. Can I hurt him just a little?"

"We ain't in charge, just make sure the person who wants him alive isn't crazier that you," Boo says, and Isaac smiles, leaning in, and the fucker bites down hard on Ajax's ear. He spits his lobe to the ground, blood pouring from the side of Ajax's head as he screams.

"Fuck, Street Rat, tell these fuckers who I am."

I close the distance between us. "You were my rival, always have been, always will be. We had an understanding.

We co-existed, but you fucked with the wrong family. You killed the mafia boss."

His face pales, and he back pedals into Isaac. "I wasn't told they were mafia, I fucking swear."

"No point having loose lips now. I have someone who really wants to talk to you," Isaac says with a maniac laugh.

One of the men Genie sent comes over to us. "Everything here is sorted, and the clean-up crew will be here shortly. We will take the bodies and deal with them. Tell Jaz when she is ready, she can be in contact."

He hands me a card, it's plain white with just a number on it, no name or details. I pocket it and watch as he walks away and gets into the white van.

"I can't die, Street Rat, I have a family. Please don't let them kill me."

Turning back to face Ajax, Boo is already on it. "You should have thought about that, but we will make sure Sunny and the kids are looked after and we can call it even for the favor I owe you...take him away before I kill him myself."

Isaac nods and starts dragging Ajax away, but he turns back as a wicked grin spreads across his face. "Tell Genie I'll play with him a little bit, but I won't kill him. I might just cut him and stitch him back up again and again," he chuckles to himself.

I nod in agreement as mixed feelings of resentment and anger pool in my stomach.

"Let's get to the hospital and help Genie," Boo says. I know that he is worried about him, Boo won't ever admit it, but I think he might be a little obsessed with this guy.

I pull out my phone and dial his number. "Where are you?"

"The one in Kingston Village, the Bianchi family doctors are all here. We didn't have time to go to the one in Willowdale, Armando was fucking bleeding from his stomach and passing out from the blood loss."

"Fuck, everything here is sorted, and Isaac has Ajax, he is taking him somewhere. We'll be there shortly."

Genie ends the call, and Boo and I head out to his beaten-up pile of junk. He jumps into the driver's side through the window now that the door doesn't open. The second that my door is closed, he peels out of the lot and onto the road. Neither of us speak the entire drive; in times like this, there really isn't much anyone can say.

He pulls into the loading bay, and we both rush into the building and through to the emergency room.

Genie stands beside a set of double doors, and he runs his blood-encrusted hands through his hair, worry etched on his face.

Boo storms over to him and wraps his arms around his waist as Genie rests his head on Boo's shoulder.

"How are they?" I ask when I reach them.

"Jaz is in with her mom. She has some bruises and surface wounds, and they are checking her over. Also, Armando is in surgery right now, and I don't know how the hell I am supposed to tell them about..."

Genie's face contorts into pain as sobs break free from his otherwise steel Façade. Boo pulls him in tighter and comforts him as best he can. I pace the floor while we wait, everyone else in the room must sense danger because they all sit on the opposite side of the room.

A huge burly man that I recognize as Mrs. Bianchi's head of security steps through the double doors. He scans the room until his gaze falls to Genie.

"She wants to see you."

Boo and Genie pull apart, and Boo takes his tattooed hand in his. We all follow the man through the back, nurses jumping out of their way as he approaches them. He is like a steam train with one destination in his mind.

"I will be outside the door, holler if you need me." I nod at him, and we all step into the room. Jaz is sitting up, and her mom is sitting on a chair by her bed, speaking to someone in Italian on the phone.

Genie doesn't move, he just watches her. "Are you okay?" I ask, breaking the silence. She winces as she moves to look at me.

"I will live, they just roughed me up a little. Mainly bruises and a few minor cuts that the doctor fixed up."

"We are glad that you're okay."

"Someone find my husband!" Mrs. Bianchi screams down the phone.

The doctor waltzes in the room with an air of arrogance, and I can tell he is definitely the doctor on their payroll.

"Jazlyn, good news, you're free to go. Armando is in surgery now, and I assure you, he is in the best hands.

"Thank you, Doctor. Can you have someone call me when he is out of surgery so that I can be here when he wakes up? I need to get some fresh air." Genie nods as the doctor leaves the room.

"Genie," Jaz's voice is quiet as she speaks. "You're not telling me something, where is my father and brother?"

The blood drains from Genie's face, and he steps in closer and takes her hand. Before he even gets a word out, she starts shaking her head.

"No, no, no, no, no."

"I'm here," a chirpy voice says as Raj flits into the room. Everyone looks at him, and he stops dead in his tracks. "What?"

"I'm so sorry, Jaz, Mrs. Bianchi, there was nothing I could do. They were not supposed to be there. They were going to meet their men, but they were both gone before I even got there."

Mrs. Bianchi screams and falls to the floor, and Boo rushes to her side, picks her up, and pulls her to his chest.

Jaz blinks, and we all wait for her to break down. She swallows hard and nods as a tear slides down her face. Raj is by her side in a second, sliding onto the bed next to her.

"They have one of the men for questioning."

Jaz's hardened gaze locks with mine. "Take me to him," she demands.

"Baby girl, you don't need to deal with this now," Raj protests. "That's what you have those men for to get their hands dirty."

She rips her hand from his and narrows her eyes at Genie. "I said take me there, everyone can stop sheltering me. I was raised right alongside Romeo and Alex. Oh my God, did he…"

I nod my head. "I'm so sorry."

"Raj, take my mom home and call her sisters to come and be with her…Loch."

The burly man steps into the room. "Take my mom

home and make sure Raj calls my aunts. We will need to make arrangements for a funeral."

Loch nods as he steps further into the room, and Boo helps Mrs. Bianchi to her feet, where she sways slightly. Loch picks her up and cradles her in his arms.

Raj slides off the bed. "Are you sure this is a good idea?"

Jaz scoffs. "I don't question you when you fuck married housewives, so please don't question me."

Hurt laces his features, but right now, Jaz is hurting, and she is putting on a mask, one she watched her father and brother put on their entire lives. She knows what them dying means, fuck, even I know what them dying means. I'm sure there are other family members that could step up, but she won't allow that to happen, and I would be doing the same thing if I were her.

"Can I use your phone?" she asks Genie, and he hands it over without question.

"Paul, it's Jazlyn. I need security at the hospital in Kingston Village. Armando is in surgery. I also need you to assign me Papa's personal security. I am heading to The Bunker now."

She ends the call and hands the phone back to Genie. He opens his mouth, but she pins him with a look that says, *fuck with me I dare you*, and he closes it again.

"I'm going to make this very clear; I won't stop until I get vengeance for my father, he would do the same for me. So, you're all either with me or against me right now."

"I would die for you, Jaz, you know that." Genie's pained eyes bore into hers.

She takes his hands and pushes up on her tippy toes,

pressing her lips to his. I see the green-eyed monster in Boo's eyes, and I shake my head no at him.

"I hope you're willing to share him because I will cut a bitch," Boo tries to lighten the mood.

Jaz snorts. "Something tells me that this is going to be fun." She looks at me and smirks. "Are you walking away Street Rat or are you in?"

"I was in the second my head was between your legs, eating your cunt." Boo makes an audible gagging sound. "You trapped me with your voodoo pussy."

"And just so you all know, I am still engaged to Armando, and it will stay that way for now. A lot of men will not respect me and having him by my side will help."

"Have fun explaining this to him," Genie says, and Boo snorts.

"I'll do it, ruffling his feathers is fun, but for now, let's go and torture a motherfucker and get some answers."

We all pile in, and Genie drives us in his Range Rover. When she said The Bunker, I figured that it was in her house, but no, this place in in the middle of fucking nowhere, and it's an underground bunker. She leads the way which indicates that she knows what goes on here.

"Marcus," she says, greeting a man in a suit that guards the door. "Thank you for coming."

If Marcus knows about Salvatore, he doesn't say anything, but he would have to be an idiot to not know.

"If there is anything you need just let me know. I have spoken with Loch and put extra security on the house, and I have my best men here today."

"I appreciate it."

He gives a nod in acknowledgement, then opens the

door, and we enter the bunker. It's not a basic doomsday thing that you would see on my side of town. No, this has some cells right as you walk in, an area that looks like a living room, a small kitchenette, and a long hall that has doors all the way along it.

Screams fill the air, and Jaz holds her head up high as she walks down the hall. About halfway down, she opens the door, and we all follow behind her. Surprisingly, the room is a lot bigger than I expected. It's big enough that we all fit in it comfortably, and everything in here feels sterile.

Ajax is hanging from the ceiling by a chain that's linked onto a hook. His shirt has been removed and blood drips down his torso. "Just in time," Isaac chirps, twirling a blade in his fingers. "He has just woken up. Take a look at my stitches, I should have become a doctor." He chuckles darkly at his own joke.

Jaz doesn't say anything, she just stands and stares at Ajax with a blank expression. None of us say anything, but we watch her as she watches him. Her hands start to tremble, and her knees give away, Genie catches her before she falls.

"Awe, the mafia princess doesn't have the guts to get the job done."

I see red. "Lucky for her, she has an army of men at her disposal."

I throw a punch into his gut, and he laughs. "The Russians are going to have fun with you. They removed a family once before, and they can do it again. And the hilarious part is, it's come to a complete circle. It all started with two men loving the same woman, and it seems it will end the same way."

"What the fuck do you mean?" Genie booms. Ajax laughs manically.

"Don't you see? Your mother was with the Italians and the Russians. Yet she married a Barber. Salvatore may have let that slide, but the Russians didn't."

Isaac passes Genie a Glock, and Genie doesn't hesitate, he pulls the trigger with Jaz tucked into his side. If any of this has any truth in it, we just uncovered a can of worms and not one that we want to open.

CHAPTER TWENTY-ONE

Jazlyn

I sit in the Rolls Royce as it idles outside the church doors. My heart pounds inside my chest as I contemplate leaving and never returning. I can't allow myself to think too much or I'll break, and a mafia Don does not break.

"Thank you, Papa, for bringing me up like you. For teaching me to be strong even when it hurts too much," I whisper into the cold air.

My driver stands outside my door waiting for my signal to open it and help me out onto my shaking legs. My mom is already sitting in the pews. She arrived at the viewing early, her eagerness marred by my absence. I couldn't look at them both laying helpless in their coffins. I need to remember them as the strong and brave men they were.

Life isn't fucking fair. I know being in this family means our days are numbered, but why did it have to be Romeo? He was supposed to be in this position, holding the family together and ruling us all. But, instead, here I am, the second choice, having to do what I never wanted to.

"I'll make you both proud." I swallow the golf ball-sized lump in my throat before I tap on the glass for the driver to let me out.

I climb out and adjust my black pencil dress and stare at my black leather pumps as they stand out against the light concrete sidewalk. The church invites me in with its open doors and whispers soothing melodies from the organ. *Left foot. Right foot*, I repeat in my head as I take the tentative steps up the pathway and close the distance between my old life and my new world.

I walk slowly down the red carpeted walkway, past grieving family and friends of my Papa's and brother's, all here to celebrate their lives. I don't dare look at anyone, but I feel the eyes of everyone I pass on me. Their pitiful stares soak into my thick skin as I take my seat beside my mom and Raj. Her soft and quiet sobs haven't stopped since the day in the hospital. I didn't think one could cry this much, and my heart bleeds for her losing both a son and a husband at once.

"My darling." Her soft-spoken words through her sobs comfort me as she grabs my hand in hers and squeezes it.

"I love you." I rest my head on her shoulder like I used to when I was a little girl, sitting right here through Sunday service every week. "It's you and me against the world."

"I love you, sweetheart," she whispers as the church organs stop, and the hushed voices of the guests fill the vaulted ceiling of the church.

The whole thing passes in a blur as the priest reads the final prayer and the word Amen echoes through the room. I stand with everyone else and follow the crowds outside, I'm the last one to leave through the church doors. It's as though everything is muted, and all I can hear is the steady beat of my heart deep in my chest. I haven't spoken a word to a single soul the whole ceremony, and no one dares come to me to give their heartfelt condolences.

A hand presses against my lower back as I stand just outside the doors and keep a watchful eye on my men who have all taken their places around the perimeter. I turn to gaze up at Genie and offer him a small smile. I know he's broken on the inside, but he too, just like me, needs to put on a brave face.

In the private confines of my bathroom, I let myself cry quietly to ease some of the built-up pressure that feels like it's going to tear me in half any day now. The deep-rooted hurt and hatred I feel consumes my every waking moment, but I know I need to keep my head level and in the game. This family won't run itself, and they are all depending on me to carry the legacy that was Salvatore Bianchi.

"Are you okay?" Genie whispers into my hair as he leans in and kisses me on the side of my head.

"No," I say truthfully as I continue to stare out into the crowd of mourners. Every made man and his dog is in attendance, showing their respects. Even the mafia Dons of other territories have come to show allegiance. None have approached me, respectfully, but I know there will be a meeting in the coming days that I will have to attend.

"I can get you out of here, just say the word." Genie grips my hand in his, and I wonder what others think when they see us so close.

"Let's just get this fucking shit over with. I need to get out of these shoes." I glance up at him and stare into his beautiful eyes. I know he blames himself for all of this, even though he couldn't prevent it even if he tried to. They would have found me and taken me at any opportunity they had.

Genie pulls me after him through the crowd. I smile and nod at each of the guests as I pass them, and they stare back at me with sympathy. One tiny, gray-haired Nonna grabs my hand in hers and gazes up at me with tears in her eyes.

"He was a good man, Bella. You will do him proud." She kisses my hand gently before letting it go.

"Thank you," I say as the breath in my lungs constricts, and I find it hard to breathe all of a sudden.

She nods in encouragement as I'm whisked away and led to the waiting cars. My mom sits in the first car all on her own, with nothing but her sorrow and thoughts. It's tradition, and as much as I want to go comfort her, I know my place is in the car behind. She needs this time and space to process the finality of all this. Only close family are permitted to watch the coffin be lowered into the ground, and as we all head to the family's crypt in the city's cemetery, I can't help but think that the eyes of our rivals are upon us the whole time.

The gloom of a cloudy day adds to my misery as I step out of the car and make my way across the wet grass to the Bianchi crypt. My heels sink into the wet dirt, and the irony of it all makes me chuckle.

"What are you thinking?" Genie eyes me carefully.

I glance up at him and smile. "Just the sinking of my heels is like the burying of my family, only I get to yank my shoe back out. I think I'm losing my mind." I squint up at him as the drizzle of the cold rain sprinkles over my face, no doubt smudging my eye makeup.

His hand tightens around my waist as we trudge through the muddy ground until we reach the large doors of the crypt. The beautiful marble is aged, and moss covers parts of it that don't get much sunlight. All our family is housed here. Their final resting place to spend eternity together. Generations of Bianchi's all coexist wherever they all go after death. It's kind of reassuring that I will one day be reunited with my brother and Papa.

My mom sobs in the corner of the small area for mourners. Armando comforts her as he stares at the two coffins in the center of the small space. I walk toward my mom and grip her around the shoulders as she buries her face in my dress.

"Shh, it's okay. They're at peace." I try to reassure her even though my own heart has split in two, and the sharp ache in my chest reminds me of our loss.

There are no other family members alive to witness the ending. Those back in the motherland were unable to attend due to not being permitted into this country for their criminal pasts. So, my mom and I say goodbye with the two men that my Papa and brother trusted most.

The priest enters in his robe, holding a large wooden cross and gently smiles at us. He begins his hymns as we stand and listen to his haunting voice. I'm sure this moment in time will be forever ingrained in my DNA.

"Amen," we all say in unison, and the sound echoes in the marble chamber.

My father and brother are lined up with their respective final resting places and slowly pushed into their crypts for eternity. The closing of the small doors is a finality that will forever haunt my nightmares.

My mom stops sobbing at that point, and I look down at her, her face is serene and calm. The events of the past week have aged her. "Let's go, Mom." I grip her shoulders and lead her back outside where the rain has increased to a steady shower.

Genie and Armando offer to hold umbrellas over us, but I shake my head at them. My mom and I need the cleansing of the rain to shower over us as we slowly make our way back to the waiting cars. Fuck tradition in this instance, and I climb in after her into her car and comfort her on our way to the wake to mingle with friends and celebrate what was Salvatore's and Romeo's life.

I stand at the edge of the grand ballroom and stare at the people here. Mobsters and crooks mingling with dignitaries and CEOs of respected top-tier businesses, all here because at one point or another, they had dealings with my family. It amuses me that they've come to pay their respects to two men they feared yet respected.

I spot Street Rat and Boo as they stalk across the room toward me, their movements lithe and cautious, always on high alert. Street Rat's gaze collides with mine, and I am momentarily taken by his raw power and big dick energy. If anyone could manipulate a crowd, it would be him.

He walks straight up to me and slides his hands to my waist, making my heart stutter. The things this man does to my insides is fucking embarrassing. Without a word, he leans in and kisses me passionately, our tongues chase one another, not giving a fuck who can see us. I'm past caring what others think. This is my world now, and if anyone has a fucking problem with how I conduct my business, I'll personally blow their heads off.

He breaks the kiss and stares into my soul. "Hi."

I swallow the need to have him inside me right at this point. "Hi."

"Get a fucking room," Boo chimes in and plants a kiss on my cheek.

"Only if you'll come too?" I turn my gaze toward him and grin.

"All over you, baby. I'll come all over you any day." He winks at me, making me laugh.

"Where's Genie and Jaffa?" Street Rat steps away from me and scans the room.

"Somewhere here. I lost sight of them a few moments ago, there was something they had to go attend to." I shrug.

Chaos erupts at that moment as gunshots ring through the otherwise still air. The crowd melts into one as they all scramble to get the fuck out before their lives are ended. The blur of movement stills me, and I watch for what seems like ages before I'm tackled sideways and pinned to the floor under someone. I blink away the pain in my side from hitting the hard floor, and as my vision clears, I see the stunning face of my savior.

"Armando," I say, confused as to what the fuck is going on.

"Don't move, baby. I'll get you out as soon as I'm given the go ahead." His face is serene and calm which calms my nerves.

"I need to help." I struggle under him. Thought of my mom out there somewhere getting injured causes my anxiety to kick up a notch.

"I don't fucking think so. This isn't your fight to have. Leave it to Genie and your men."

The noise surrounding us is deafening as the gunfire and screams all meld into one. My heart constricts at the thought of any of them getting hurt, and I try to climb out from under Armando's weight, but he grips my wrists in his strong hands and stops me.

"A few more seconds." He stares deep into my eyes to try to convince me not to draw attention to us.

"Fuck, I can't just stay here and let this happen. I need to find my mom. Who the fuck is attacking us?"

"The Russians," Armando whispers before his body weight is lifted off me, and he grips me by the waist and hauls me to my feet.

I'm half carried out of the mayhem that has erupted in the beautiful ballroom of this swanky hotel. This will be a nice bill once the damages are calculated.

"Let go of me!" I struggle in Armando's grip, and his hands disappear once we're out the back of the building.

I try to get back inside, but he grabs me and holds me against him. "Your mom is safe, she was taken out before the shooting started," he soothes as his hands rub against my back.

"So, what now? I can't just stay out hcrc hiding. What will that look like as the new Don of the family?" I question him, annoyed that I'm not in amongst the murdering of these fucking coward bastards. Who the fuck shoots up a fucking wake?

Armando grips my jaw in his fingers and angles my face up to his. "It's already over. Your men have done what they're paid to do."

The gun shots have ceased but the screaming and shouting continue as our friends try to flee. My heart aches for any victims who have been killed in the crossfire. I will no doubt pay for this fuckery for years to come. The doors we escaped through fly open and out rush Street Rat, Genie, and Boo. I leap into Genie's arms, and he cradles me against his muscled chest. I can feel the rapid beat of his heart as he catches his breath. I pull away from him and check him over to make sure he hasn't been shot.

"Hey, we're all okay." He takes my hands in his and makes me focus on him. "Everything is going to be okay, I promise."

"Take her upstairs, we will help with the clean-up down here."

"I need to help."

All four pin me with a glare. "You're all this family has left, Jaz," Armando snaps. "Get her to safety, now!"

I pull away from Genie, he can't force me to leave, except he is double my size, and he picks me up over his shoulder and takes me upstairs, two at a time. He pulls out a swipe card and opens a door and the door shut behind us.

"You need to let me out," I demand, and he throws me down onto my bed.

"No."

"It's an order, let me leave."

He bellows out a laugh. "Baby girl, I don't work for you. I worked for your father, and I work for Armando, and he ordered me to bring you up here. You two can figure that out later. For now, get naked."

My mouth falls open. "I didn't stutter, Princess, get naked now!"

He loosens his tie and pulls it over his head and throws it to the floor. "If I have to remove your clothes, I will spank your ass."

I lay there stunned; I can't do this now with everyone downstairs. His shirt is next to be removed, and his entire torso is filled with tattoos. His belt next and he does that sexy one move, and the belt is thrown toward the bed. The next thing I know he is naked and crawling up the bed, hovering over top of me.

"You have been a bad girl, and now I plan to punish you."

My pussy clenches at his words, and everything going on downstairs is momentarily forgotten.

"On all fours."

I nod, and he pushes up, leaning back on his legs. He waits and watches me turn over, still fully clothed. Once I'm in position, he slides the dress over my ass, and he groans. I look back at him, and he is biting down on his knuckle.

"Fuck, you're beautiful. I wish the others could see you like this. Now, take this and bite down, no one gets to hear you scream."

He hands me his belt, and once it's between my teeth, he brings his hand down on my ass, hard. The pain centers me, and as all the overwhelming feelings start to boil to the surface, tears spring to my eyes.

His hand comes down again and again until he is done, and he presses soft kisses to my ass cheek.

"You're perfect, look at how wet you are for me."

The belt drops from my mouth as he moves up behind me. "This is going to be hard and fast; I have imagined how our first time alone would be, and I don't have time to worship your body now."

I glance over my shoulder, and he palms his massive cock and presses it against my slit, moving it around my juices, lubing himself up. Once he pushes the head inside me, he twists his hand into my hair and pulls my head back and slams himself balls deep inside me. I scream, feeling the ribbed sensation send shockwaves through my body.

"Can you feel that, the barbells sliding over your g-spot?"

He thrusts into me, and I do feel them, every single one, but it's coming from both sides.

"Fuck," he growls. "I don't know who takes my cock better, you or Boo."

"Don't stop," I pant. "Please don't stop."

My world spins every time he pulls back, he doesn't relent. He fucks me hard like he promised until I'm a quivering mess, and I'm screaming his name. Every single inch of my skin tingles from the shock waves that exploded over my body.

Once he finishes and pulls out, my body drops to the bed, and I curl up into a ball, and he slides in behind me and pulls my body to his. "Let it all out, Jaz, you're allowed to grieve and to feel in this room. With me, with us, because we will all be there for you every step of the way. But you're allowed to take some time. You lost your father, your brother, and a good friend. You need to feel it because this life isn't easy. Your enemies will always be lurking in the background, and you need to be smart, so if we tell you to leave, you need to. It's not because you're a woman, we would have done the same for your father. It's our job to protect the head of the family. With the Russians after us, please promise me you will listen."

"I promise to try."

He holds me while I cry, losing them all is something I knew was a possibility, but I never expected to be a reality. The thought of having to fill their shoes terrifies me. But he is right. First, I need to grieve, and everything else can wait.

CHAPTER TWENTY-TWO

Jazlyn

No one should ever have to attend funerals for three people within days of each other. Alex's parents held a small funeral for him. His mother refused to let anyone connected with the mafia in, except me. I couldn't take Armando or Genie with me because of their affiliation, and neither of them would let me go unless I had someone with me. So, Street Rat and Boo came along to make sure I was safe.

"Jazlyn, are you listening to me?" Armando asks. I look up from my Papa's desk and shake my head no.

"Sorry, I know we have to have that meeting. I just don't know if I'm ready yet."

Jaffa stands and comes around the desk, spins my chair, and squats down in front of me, his hands landing on my thighs. "I know how this started with us and it was a means to an end, then I saw you with those Stronzo's, and it did something to me. Those men in that room today will know you're mine. If they don't respect you, there will be war between us."

"What if I can't make Papa proud?"

I know that it's stupid, I watched them for years and listened when they didn't think I would be. Mom even took me to self-defense lessons and the shooting range. She wanted me prepared, maybe not for this role, but she would always say loving a powerful man comes with the dangers of his lifestyle."

The door flies open, and Boo waltzes in. "It's time to get naked," he says. I glance up and snort, he is already as naked as the day he was born except for a bright orange pair of socks.

"What? This house is full of tiles and my feet get cold."

"Where is Mrs. Bianchi?" Armando asks.

"She has gone to a wellbeing retreat, she needed to get away. And buddy, my eyes are up here."

I snort as Genie steps into Papa's office, and he is also naked. "What the fuck?! Why are you all naked? This isn't a brothel."

"We need to strong arm you, buddy, we know you won't come willingly."

Armando stands from his squatting position in front of me, and I pull my piece from the back of my pants suit and hold it to his temple.

"Jazlyn," he warns. "Don't make me hurt you."

"Don't underestimate me, Jaffa, start walking."

I know he could unarm me in a second if he wanted to, I know he is curious about what I have with the others. He just has too much pride, so I decided to make it easier for him, except these idiots were not supposed to be naked.

"Where am I walking to exactly?"

"Follow us, pretty boy, but don't stare at my man's ass," Boo jokes, slapping Genie's ass as we walk out and through the foyer.

Armando follows the guys up the stairs and down the hall to my room, where Street Rat is, thankfully clothed. He shakes his head at Genie and Boo.

"Thank God, if I had to watch Boo suck Genie's cock again, I may have considered letting him suck mine. You got the big man to agree to join us, and I foresee one of us not making it through this."

"That's where you're wrong," I say. "Armando, weapons on the floor, now."

Armando is quiet as he unstraps his weapons and lays them all on the floor.

"Don't forget the knife strapped to your leg," Genie says, and Armando smirks, removing the knife.

He isn't stupid, once the knife is gone, he sits in the chair we brought up here from the basement. I doubt it's ever been used for sexual purposes, but it has been used to torture men. Boo laughs when he watches Armando strap himself in.

"You keen to watch me fuck our girl? Tell me what you want to see," Boo teases.

"Fuck you," Jaffa seethes through clenched teeth. "I'm not doing this for you, and the verdict is still out on whether or not I slit your throat when we are done."

Standing in front of Armando, I make sure that his wrist and ankle straps are correctly clicked closed, then I lean down and unbutton his shirt as I feel his gaze burn my skin. I yank his shirt so that it untucks from his slacks.

"Don't pull my cock out in front of them."

I laugh. "Jaffa, I don't think you're in charge anymore. Relax and let me make you feel good."

His teeth grind together, and he jerks on his arms as I undo his belt and unbutton his slacks, sliding my hand in beneath his boxer briefs. He hisses as my hand wraps around his length.

"I don't know if I can watch them fuck you, you're mine."

I lean in and let my lips sit just above his. "That's the thing, I can dictate my own story now. Those men over there mean just as much to me as you do. I don't know how this will work, or if it even will, but I want to live *my* life, not the one written for me. If, once we are done here, it's not for you then you can walk away from us. I still want you as the underboss; if anyone can take Romeo's place, it's you."

He nods, he understands why I'm doing this.

"I think that you're wearing too many clothes," Boo says, coming to stand behind me. He pulls me to my feet and unbuttons my blouse, but my eyes never leave Armando. Genie and Street Rat don't think that he will be able to handle it, but Boo thinks once my pussy is wrapped around his cock, he will change his mind. I have known Armando for a very long time, and the man I know would probably have a bullet with their names on it already, but the last few weeks, something has changed.

My shirt drops to the floor, and Boo unzips my pencil skirt. I was going to wear this to the meeting we have later today.

"I need to touch you," Armando groans, and Boo runs his hand across my stomach.

"Like this?" he asks. "Or what If I do this?"

Boo slides his hand beneath my lace panties. "I'm going to kill you," Armando seethes, pulling at his restraints. "You're a dead man walking. I'm going to cut off your hands first."

"Can you shut him up already? Stuff her underwear in his mouth."

Boo laughs at Street Rat, and I turn to see that he is now also naked. Boo slides my lace underwear down my legs, and I step out of them. Boo comes around and stands in front of Armando.

"Open wide, so I can come inside," he sing-songs.

Armando thrashes his head to the side. "Get your cock away from me."

"Chill dude, I'm just letting you taste her sweet pussy juices first."

Boo grabs his face and shoves my panties in his mouth. "Damn, have you all seen how white his teeth are? Do you have some kind of trick?"

"Boo," Genie warns.

Armando uses his tongue to push the material from his mouth, but Boo isn't having it. He finds one of my material headbands and uses that to secure them in place. Once he is done, he steps back to admire his handy work.

"Now be a good boy and don't move. Let's show you how we fuck."

I yip as Street Rat comes up behind me and scoops me up into his arms and takes me over to the bed. My knees fall apart the moment he lays me down, and Boo pushes everyone aside and jumps onto the bed, his head going straight between my thighs. I am laying across my bed sideways, and when I turn my head, I can see Armando as he watches on with curiosity.

Boo's tongue pushes inside me, my hips buck, and my hands fall to his head as I grind against his face. Genie steps up beside the bed, cutting off my view of Armando.

"Lube this up well." He grins as he strokes his large hand over his already rock-hard cock.

I nod, and he steps closer, kneeling with one knee on the bed as his hand moves behind my head and helps lift it from the bed so I can suck him in, running my tongue over all his piercings.

"Fuck, your mouth is amazing."

Before I can get to into it, he pulls out of my mouth and moves off the bed, going to stand behind Boo.

I lock eyes with Armando again. "Tell Jaffa how much you like Boo eating your cunt," Street Rat says.

"I fucking love it, he eats me like a starved man."

Boo pulls his head back and grins up at me. "Now he gets to watch us stretch you open."

Street Rat jumps up onto the bed, and he pats his lap as he rolls a condom down his length, and I arch a brow. "As much as I want to fuck you raw and watch Genie eat it from that perfect cunt, we need to ease the other one into that, and he gets to fuck you last."

"No, if he wants in, this is how it's going to be. I'm in charge."

Street Rat laughs and pulls the latex from his cock and flings it to the side with a smirk on his face.

Moving up the bed, I straddle his waist, and he slides

into me gently, his eyes closing as bliss washes over his face. I love knowing that it's me that does that to him. Boo quickly moves up behind me.

"This will be cold. Princess," he says, squirting lube on my ass.

"If we have lube, why did I..."

Genie laughs, "I just wanted your mouth on my cock before I put it in his ass."

I shake my head. "You could have just said so, I would have let you put it in my pussy."

A sound vibrates from his chest, and before I know what's happening, I have been pulled from Street Rat, and Genie is slamming into me from behind, a scream peeling from my lips. "Fuck, I love those piercings," I say as my walls clamp around him.

After a few thrusts, he pulls out, and I climb back onto Street Rat. I look into his eyes to make sure he is okay with this, and he nods, gripping my hips and guiding me back onto his cock. Boo takes his place and runs his cock up my crack, spreading the lube around.

"Deep breath, beautiful. Street Rat finally gets to touch my dick."

Street Rat shakes his head at Boo, and I even my breathing as Boo pushes inside me. Neither man moves straight away.

"Fuck," Boo screams. "I'm sorry, Princess, but I'm going to blow my load a few times, his cock does amazing things to me."

Genie thrusts into Boo, and that causes a chain reaction to us all moving together. Everything around me vanishes, and I just feel. Street Rat's hands on my waist, Boo's lips against my back, and the sweat that starts to drip from my forehead. Even Genie's fingertips that keep lightly brushing against my skin.

My nipples are hard and could cut glass and my orgasm builds. "I'm going to come," I moan as shock waves shoot through my body.

"You look beautiful when you come. Enough, I'm going to join you."

Street Rat shudders from beneath me. "Oh fuck, right there don't stop," Boo says before his fingers dig into my sides, and his cock thickens in my ass.

One by one, they all move from me, and I flop down onto the bed. Genie picks me up and cradles me to his chest like I am his greatest treasure. "You're not done, Princess. You need to show this one who is boss."

Genie places me on my feet before a still tied-up Armando, and I turn, sitting on his lap, his hard cock pressing between my ass cheeks. I pull my legs up and spread them; a smile is on Genie's face, and Boo is beside him. "Wanna eat our girl's pussy before she fucks him stupid?" Boo asks Genie. Both men fall to their knees in front of me, Boo leans in first and licks my slit, and then when he pulls back, Genie replaces him. They take turns to lick and suck until my body trembles beneath them. Just as another orgasm rips through me and wetness pools beneath me.

"Fuck, that's hot," Boo says, pulling back.

He helps me stand, and this time, I straddle Armando's lap and rip the headband from his mouth, then pull my panties out.

"You need to fuck me now," he demands, and I reach

my hand between us and pull his cock from his pants and sink down on it. Resting my hands on his shoulders, I grind against him.

"Kiss me?" he asks, and I smirk at him. Armando usually demands that you do something, but the slight pause and his tone indicates for the first time ever he is asking me. Leaning forward, I press my breasts against his chest, we're as close as we could possibly get, and I press my lips against his, pushing my tongue into his mouth.

And that's how we make love for the first time, as close as two people can get with him cuffed to a chair, and my pussy and ass full of other men's come.

CHAPTER TWENTY-THREE

Jaffa

I never imagined in my wildest dreams that I would have been turned on watching other men fuck what's mine. There were multiple times I wished I had a weapon in my hand, but something clicked, and when I saw the pure bliss on her face, my traitorous cock was hard as stone.

"Do I look okay?" Jaz asks, as Genie opens the door to the Range Rover.

"You're perfect, and if you need to circle the block again, I could make the nerves disappear."

She chuckles, "You are a fiend, Jaffa. One gang bang, and you can't keep your hands off me."

"What can I say, you unlocked a kink I didn't know I had. But mark my words, any other man beside them touches you, and they will die. I will skin them alive and let the weird one wear it as a suit."

"Boo isn't weird."

"That's debatable," I say, stepping out of the vehicle. I would have much preferred to drive myself here, but this car is bullet proof, and we can't take any risks with the Russians breathing down my neck.

Thanks to that low life gang banger, we know that this all stems back to a rift between the Italians and Russians many years ago over Genie's mother. If you had told me this a week ago, I would have sided with the Russians. I would have wanted to hunt down those fuckers' families and killed them all as punishment for touching what's mine, and then I would have saved her for last. But losing Salvatore and Romeo has put things into perspective. I have to protect Jazlyn at all costs, even if that means she has four cocks in her daily. I can live with that if I am one of those four. I swore an oath to the Bianchi family. Just as every other man standing on this sidewalk has done, including Street Rat and Boo. We met with the family last night, and while some had reservations about Jaz taking over, we have assured them that she will be fine with me by her side and Isaac as her consigliere. I would have thought that she would have chosen Genie, but it makes no sense for him to go from her security to consigliere overnight. No one would have gone for that, and she knows it.

Today we have a meeting with the families and others we have an alliance with. We need to make sure that we are all on the same page. Salvatore would have promised things that Jaz might not be comfortable with.

We all move into the building quickly; if we stand out here for much longer, we are sitting ducks.

Jazlyn leads the way into the building dressed in a power suit that hugs her ass, and I can't wait to peel them from her body. After what Boo classed as a gang bang, we did all sit down at my request. I know she wants this to work, and I will do whatever it takes to make her happy as per my promise to her father. I don't think I will be down for group sex often, but watching her with them wasn't as bad as I thought. I may even be okay with sharing her with Genie, but that street scum can stay away from me. We came to an agreement that we won't kill each other, and even though I know I will regret it, I am a man of my word.

Entering the room, men are seated around a large oval table, one representative from each family waiting for our arrival, and I can see the questions in their eyes. They all stand as Jaz walks into the room.

"Gentleman, take your seats. Firstly, I want to thank you all for your kind words at my father and Romeo's funeral."

I run my eyes around the room; I trust none of these men, and Jazlyn has been told not to either. We don't know how anyone will handle a woman being in charge. The Irish mob sent a young guy, someone that I have not met formally. I know his name is Finn, but beyond what a police check can tell you, I don't know why his uncle isn't here, and it doesn't sit right with me.

"So, are we going to address the elephant in the room?" he asks. Jazlyn looks over at him as if she was totally bored. Good girl, don't let these men see fear on your face.

"And what elephant might that be, hmm? That I'm a woman? Is that the issue because I don't have a chunk of meat between my legs?" She leans down on the table and levels her eyes with his. "If you have an issue with me being a woman, then you need to see yourself to the door. I came here today in good faith that we could talk like adults. I plan to honor the peace agreements that you all made with my father. Armando has brought me up to speed, but before we go any further, this is your chance to leave."

"How can we trust that you can be trusted?"

"I understand that you're all worried, I'm new and stepping into big shoes, but you have my word."

The Irish guy scoffs, "Your word means shit, lady, we don't know you. We haven't worked with you so how we are supposed to trust you?"

The door swings open, and every man in the room whips their guns out as Isaac strolls in with something bloody in his hands. He throws it at the table, and the slab of meat hits it.

"Another Russian bites the dust," he cackles. "Sorry I'm late, Princess. I had a lead and well the lead is dead. Gentleman."

Isaac nods his head, and the men sit up a little straighter in their chairs. They understand how unhinged this man is. He doesn't ask questions first; he kills and finds the answers himself.

"I hope everyone has been respectful in my absence. Armando?"

I nod toward Finn, and Isaac turns with a questioning brow raised. Finn holds up his hands in a placating manner. "Wait a second, we have a right to be concerned."

"You don't have a right to feel fuck all. She has done nothing to make you question her, and to top it all off, she has Armando and I at her side."

I roll my lips over my teeth. Jaz specifically told us that we couldn't talk for her and to not get involved unless things became dangerous. We were naked when she asked, and I was backed into a corner.

"Isaac!"

"Yes, Love?" he says, turning and facing her with a wide smile. "Are you done?"

"Almost."

He walks around the table and places his hands in Finn's shoulders, the blood on his hands now transferred to Finn's T-shirt. Serves the fucker right for wearing something with holes in it to this meeting.

Isaac leans in close to Finn's ear and whispers something. "Now I'm done."

No one else says anything, it's not their family, nor their business. Every man in this room is out for themselves. They can't afford a war with us or our men, and not to mention that innocent lives will get lost if they decide to try.

Jazlyn takes over and talks to all the men in the room and assures them that she will be in contact at a later date. Most of the men in the room are too old to want to start trouble. We have lived peacefully for years, and they don't plan to start raising issues now. The Irish must be close to a change over for Finn to be here, and I know Salvatore worked hard to get them on our side. Only time will tell if they still side with us over the Russians, but I feel like Isaac drove the point home.

When the meeting comes to an end, I tell Genie to take Jazlyn home, and that I will be there after I finish some business. I sit and wait patiently until the three dipshits have taken my girl home.

Standing, I shrug my jacket off and place it down neatly on the chair I just vacated, and I roll the sleeves of my crisp white button-down shirt up to the elbows. I rarely show the world my tattoos, they are private, and I don't feel the need to have them to make me look tough. I know what I can do and what I am capable of. Isaac shakes his head at me and smiles. He knows what is about to happen. Finn is chatting with some of the men at the table, none of whom look impressed by his actions.

Walking around the back of the table, some would say it's cowardly to catch a man off guard. I would say that he should be alert at all times in a room full of mobsters.

Grabbing the back of his head, I slam it into the table and step back. He jumps from his chair with a painful groan as blood pours from his nose.

"What the fuck was that for?" he demands.

"That, my friend, was for disrespecting my woman. You know that we are engaged to be married, and you still disrespected her in front of me."

"And you want my loyalty," he spits, blood now pooling in his hand.

"I don't need your loyalty, not you or any of the men in the room, because something you don't seem to grasp is none of these men here are loyal to anyone but themselves. That is how this world works. We have a truce at best. Our family doesn't have any beef with your families, and we want to keep it that way. I don't particularly like spilling blood, unlike Isaac who lives for it. We don't need any innocent lives lost. Salvatore, Romeo, and Alex were not innocent, but you have wives and children, and those are the people who get hurt and don't deserve it."

"The question you need to ask yourself, Finn, is do we have a problem here because the Armando I know would have put a bullet through your head, but as it seems, he is pussy-whipped."

The older men in the room all laugh, and I grind my teeth together. I'm not pussy whipped, I just know my place, and if I kill Finn, it'll bring drama to our doorstep the first week in her father's role. She may just kill me herself or get one of her little boyfriends to do it. I hope one day she wakes up and realizes that she doesn't want them, but her father isn't here to force her to be with me and that leaves me with having to compete with them.

"No," Finn says. "You won't have any problems from me. Now, if you don't mind, I have to go home to my woman."

I scratch my face. "Don't ever tell a room full of your enemies that you're going home to your woman. It's different for me since mine is in a position of power."

He nods and leaves the room.

"Gentleman, if we are done here, I have a club to check up on. You're all welcome to join me in the VIP room of The Lamp, you just have to find it first."

With that, I leave them, grabbing my jacket on my way past with Isaac on my tail.

"So, you finally found The Lamp," Isaac says with a chuckle.

"Not by myself. He couldn't have made it any harder to find. Now I get to run it how I see fit."

"If I didn't know any better, I would think that you were happy Salvatore was dead."

I cut a glare to him and narrow my eyes. "Don't ever say that shit out loud again. Of course I'm not fucking happy.

Working for him was what I wanted in life and to marry his daughter."

Isaac slips into the passenger side of my Ferrari, and we cruise the streets until we come to an underground garage, one only we have access to along with our security for The Lamp.

I may have gotten the location, but at what cost? Salvatore, one of the main men who shaped me into the person that I am today, is gone, and even for someone like me, it hurts to think about sometimes.

CHAPTER TWENTY-FOUR

Jazlyn

Street Rat has been putting off officially introducing us to his mom. She obviously knows Boo, and she met me briefly the first night that we ever met. And here we are exactly one year later, dressed in prosthetics from Lady Trey, ready to party on the streets of Kingston Village. Even Jaffa is here. I can't say that he is overly impressed by it. Even after this long, he is still slightly on the outside of us.

"Lalah," Boo yells as he jumps the small white picket fence. Street Rat interlocks our fingers. Genie and Armando follow behind.

"Are you sure it's okay to turn up to dinner like this? We should have dressed up," Armando whines from behind us. I don't know what he is so worked up about, he is dressed as a fucking zombie even if he is still wearing a suit.

Street Rat snorts. "Man, have a look around you, does this seem like a place where we would wear your kind of expensive Italian suits? You would be better received if you wore your pajamas."

Genie snorts from beside me. "I think he is nervous." Genie turns to look at Armando. "You are so nervous to meet his mom."

"Fuck this, I knew I shouldn't have come," he says. I drop Street Rat's hand and turn around, chasing Armando down the stairs.

"Stop."

He halts in his tracks and turns to face me. I step up to him and cup his face. "I appreciate you coming with us. I know this whole situation is hard for you, and you have been doing amazing. This is also a big step for Street Rat, allowing us to meet the most impor- tant person in his life. He is scared her meeting us involves her in our lives and that someone will hurt her."

He nods. "I'm sorry, I'm not used to being around people who don't want to be part of this life. Let's go inside before I change my mind."

By the time we go inside, Boo, Street Rat, and Genie are all seated around a small table. They all stand when I walk into the room, Street Rat's mom watches them, then stands as well.

"Mom, you don't need to stand," Street Rat says with a laugh.

"Oh, right, sorry, I forget about this whole..." She looks around and lowers her voice. "Mafia stuff."

Boo snorts. "That is also not a secret, Lalah, but in this house and neighborhood, she is just princess, a regular girl with three boyfriends and a Jaffa."

Jaffa growls behind me. "What's a Jaffa?"

"That would be me," Armando says. "Jazlyn gave me

that nickname a long time ago and unfortunately, it's stuck."

"And we spoke about this, if anyone around here asks, it's Jaffa, no one needs to know your real name. Do you want someone to steal your identity or nark on you?"

"I would just kill them," Armando says at the same time Genie jumps in and says, "With kindness, he will kill them with kindness."

We all look at Street Rat's mom, varying stages of cringe on all our faces. This is not going well, we all know it, but she just laughs. "Come everyone, sit down. I'm not an idiot, I have some basic understanding of what goes on in the mafia. I just hope you're all being safe."

She gets up from the table, and Street Rat jumps up to help her. They bring a roast to the table, the delicious smell making my stomach rumble.

Armando serves me a plate, while everyone else digs in.

"So, tell me how this works. When Street Rat told me you were in this type of relationship, I couldn't for the life of me understand, and I still don't."

I set my knife and fork down. "It's simple really, I have feelings for them all. I was told my entire life how things would work. I had to be married, I was expected to be a good wife and do as my husband says. Now that I'm in charge, I can dictate my own life, and if I don't have to choose, even better. It's not easy, that's for sure."

"That's an understatement," Armando mutters under his breath.

"What he means is, he and I were engaged to be married, but my father chose him for me. I still plan to honor my father's request, but I'm not willing to give up the others."

"Don't forget Genie is my man," Boo says through a mouthful of potatoes.

I roll my eyes. "Genie and Boo also have a sexual relationship."

Her mouth falls open. "Lalah, it's not all that complicated. She bones all of us, and then Genie bones me if I'm a good boy."

Lalah smacks Boo upside the head, and we all laugh. "Child, I don't want to know who bones whom. I just can't imagine loving more than one person."

"So, what you really mean is, you couldn't watch someone you love be boned by some..."

"Boo, stop, you're making it worse."

He laughs, "I make everything better, and tell me those barbells don't make everything right in the world."

Genie goes bright red, even Armando snorts but tries to cover it up with a napkin that he magically pulled out of nowhere.

"I don't want to know, I'm sorry I brought it up. Boo, you're just a lot sometimes, I don't even understand how you managed to get two people to be with you."

"Me either, Lalah, but I won't complain. I'm getting love from every angle."

Once Boo stops talking about our sex life, we finish our meal, and even Armando has had a good time. If he hadn't, he would be moody and complaining, but he has been in a deep conversation with Lalah about how to treat an infected wound. Can't say that the conversation really interests me, but they have been laughing. *Armando is laughing.* Hell must have officially frozen over.

Street Rat says goodbye to his mom, and we all walk into town which is set up like a massive, haunted maze. Stall holders have set up and are dressed up, people run from being chased by people in costume. The whole atmosphere is amazing.

"In here," Street Rat says, leading us into a building.

"We might not be able to chase you around the streets for your safety, but every man in this building works for us," Genie adds.

"So, you better run, Princess," Boo laughs.

"If I catch her first, she is mine for the night," Armando says.

Screw this, I run up the stairs and pull the door open to a man dressed as Frankenstein standing in the foyer. He wouldn't dare touch me, but my heart races at the thought of the guys catching me first. I open the second door, and it opens into a hallway covered in spiderwebs that look so frightening real. A shiver runs down my spine, and I take a deep breath and scream as I run all the way down, making sure to not touch anything. As I round the corner, a man with a chainsaw jumps out, and my heart beats rapidly in my chest.

"Princess," Boo calls out. I don't wait for him, but I stall at the crossroad of two halls. I look left, and its pitch black. The one on the right has a small overhead light at the end and a damn tricycle. Fuck, I watched that movie and the twins pop up. Still, I take my luck with them.

I creep down the hall, and when no one jumps out, I open a door, finding it's a room full of cages.

"You, out," I demand, pointing to a woman in a cage hanging from the roof. "Anyone else in this room that wants to keep their jobs, come out now and give me a boost."

"Yes, boss."

Head of security steps out, and I snort at his outfit. He is dressed in overalls and has on a straw hat and no shirt.

He helps the girl from the cage and gives me a boost until I pull myself in. "Now, everyone get back in place so they don't find me."

This entire plan was great in hindsight, but a few things started to happen over the course of half an hour. My legs started to go numb from being squished into a cage, and seriously, that poor girl needs a raise for being stuffed in here. So far Armando, Genie, and Boo have come through the room and not spotted me. Street Rat has yet to show his face, but the guy finds things for a living. Armando has been talking to me about making him useful to us, giving him a new role. Apparently, sex slave is the wrong answer, and Armando had me bent over his knee which he didn't realize wasn't a punishment.

"Seriously, Street Rat, you have ten minutes to find her, or I start fucking shooting people. We have checked every inch of this place."

I watch Armando walk up and down the room. "Where the fuck is she?"

Street Rat walks into the room, and Armando hangs up the phone.

"I don't know, she came through here about half an hour ago."

Street Rat's eyes follow our head of security, and he

smiles. "How about you go find the others, and I will sweep the place one last time."

Armando mumbles something and leaves the room. "It's genius really, Princess, but right now, you have some pissed off men who think you have been stolen. Boo is talking Genie off a ledge, Armando is going to start executing people who don't know where you are, your head of security just lied for you, and I saved the big man's life right now."

I laugh and open the cage door while Street Rat helps me down. "Clear the building and send them in here, please."

He leaves the room, and Street Rat levels me with a stare. "How do you feel about getting on your knees, Princess, and showing them what they are missing out on."

I drop to my knees and unbutton his jeans, pulling his cock out. I lean forward and wrap my mouth around the head, running my tongue over the pre cum that has beaded on the tip. "Fuck," he hisses as the door opens, and the guys stumble in.

"Finders keepers," Street Rat says as I suck his cock right into the back of his throat. I work his cock like it's the best damn meal I have had all week. Boo and Genie move in closer, both men pulling out their cocks.

"Come on, brother-husband, get over here and whip your cock out, there is no shame in choking the chicken in front of friends."

I snort around the hard cock in my mouth, and Armando surprises the hell out of me as he steps up close, slowly pulling his length out of his slacks. "We are not friends," he seethes.

"Brother-husbands it is."

"Stop talking or I will slap you in the face with my cock."

"Don't threaten me with a good time," Boo throws backs, and Armando growls. All three of them start jerking off above me while I suck Street Rat off in the barely lit room with cages surrounding us.

His cock thickens in my mouth, and his warm releases coats my tongue. I swallow just as the first release from one of the others hits my face.

Armando is last, and he shifts in front of me as his hand moves over his cock effortlessly. He makes it look like the most natural thing in the world. I hold my mouth open, and he comes against my lips. I lick them clean, and then he pulls me to my feet.

"We need to get you home, now; our night is just beginning."

Armando picks me up and throws me over his shoulder, his hand coming down hard on my ass, stopping the snark that is about to come from my mouth.

Boo whoops, and we all make our way out of the maze and back to the black Range Rover parked out in front of Street Rat's mom's house. Armando carries me the entire way. He refused to put me down so the cum had time to dry on my face. Maybe this man is a bit kinkier than he likes to think because for someone who claims they hate to share, he sure as shit doesn't show it with his actions.

CHAPTER TWENTY-FIVE

Jazlyn

The smooth leather of the plush office chair my Papa sat in his entire mob life cradles me as though his arms are wrapped around me, comforting me and giving me strength. This new world has welcomed me with open arms, except for the Irish. My Papa's men have all supported me and guided me through this tumultuous time of grief and loss. Their unyielding guidance and the way they've taken me under their wings will forever be etched in my mind.

A knock at the office door has me glancing up from my computer. "Come in," I say as I wait to see who will enter.

"Ciao, Jazlyn," Giuseppe says, as his bright smile beams at me. He closes the door after him and takes a seat on the other side of the large mahogany desk. He slides a large white envelope toward me and waits.

I take it and look at him. "What's this?"

"A little present for you." He smiles and waits.

I tentatively slide out the papers in the envelope. They

feel glossy on one side and smooth on the other. I know instantly they are photographs, but of what, I am not sure. I glance down at the image on the very top, and my heart jumps in my chest. A warm triumph washes over me as I take in every detail of the gruesome picture staring up at me. Tears well in my eyes as I shuffle through the remaining photographs.

I glance up at him. "Thank you," I barely whisper to the man I've known my entire life.

"Anything for you, my darling girl. You just say the word, and we'll get you the world." He nods and stands to leave.

"Thank you," is all I can say as the emotions get caught in my throat. I watch him leave the office before I stare at the photos again.

The mangled and mutilated bodies of those that murdered my brother and Papa stare back at me. Their expressionless faces show no remorse, and the feeling of wanting to dig up their bodies and butcher them rages through me. I am grateful for these tokens of what these men suffered, but my heart is not satisfied, and I will seek revenge by murdering every last member of their families to ensure they are eradicated from this earth. Torture wasn't something I ever thought I would be capable of, and it's not my most favorite pastime, but luckily I have Isaac around and willing to help teach me. Armando hates to get his hands dirty, and Street Rat and Boo have a long way to go before my father's men trust them.

I throw the photos in the desk drawer, grab my car keys, and switch off the computer. I need a stiff drink in a dank dark bar. I escape the confines of the office, jump in my car, and head to my favorite bar. One I know the bartender will bring me endless glasses of my Papa's favorite whiskey without wanting to chat with me.

I park the car, climb out, and head inside. I walk straight past the bar and seat myself in the back booth, away from any other day drinking patrons. The bartender delivers a tumbler, and the whole bottle of expensive aged whiskey. I must look like a fucking mess and in need of a stiff drink or ten. I thank him as he strides away. I have gotten used to this sort of treatment, and I fucking love it. People fear me and others worship the ground I walk on. Something I never thought I'd get a kick out of.

I pour myself a drink and slide down in the cheap, fake leather bench seat. I sip the amber liquid and enjoy the mellowness of it sliding down my throat. It's funny how I've slowly morphed into my Papa, in both my mannerisms and my thoughts. I never imagined I'd be as cut-throat as him and be happy to leave a litter of dead lives in my wake. I know people fear me. I see in their gazes before they avert their eyes from connecting with mine.

I lean my head back and close my eyes in search of a little peace in my chaotic lifestyle. Don't get me wrong, I wouldn't change it for the world now that I have it, but sometimes I think back to the carefree life of before.

I concentrate on the steady and even beat of my heart as it thrums in my chest. I'm startled by the movement of the bench seat under me. I sit up suddenly and see the eyes of my men staring back at me. Genie, Armando, Street Rat, and Boo stand over me in their sharp suits. They look fucking delicious, and I still pinch myself, not believing that they're all mine. "What are you all doing here?" I glance at each one of them before they all move to seat themselves beside me.

Boo throws back the rest of the whiskey in the glass and pours another. "We're here to talk business. The Russians are stirring again."

"What have you heard?" I sit up straighter and watch Boo with interest.

"Babe, they're just up to their old tricks. They've killed one of your soldiers' entire families, right down to his third cousins back in Italy," Genie sighs and shakes his head.

"Kill them all," I say flatly with zero emotion. My heart bleeds for my soldier and his family, and it will be over my dead body if anyone else gets murdered because of my name.

"Sorry. Say that again." Street Rat stares at me proud as fuck.

"Murder every last motherfucker associated with that fucking organization. I want their tailors, their fucking newspaper delivery guys, their corner store owners they're associated with all ended. Fuck them if they think they can keep getting away with this."

"This will start a war." Armando looks me dead in the eyes.

"Then I'll be ready and waiting."

He nods and Genie takes out his phone and puts it to his ear. "You get your wish... She sure did, find out what you can. We take action tomorrow."

He ends the call, and it's done. Tomorrow, we go after the Russians, they have been lying low since my father died, and just recently they started to target my men and their families. I won't stand for them coming after what's mine.

If they want a war, they will get one. I look up at Street Rat.

"Are you ready?" I ask him, taking a sip of the fresh glass of whiskey Armando just poured me.

"Am I ready for what?" he asks.

"To become the finder."

His brows furrow and his eyes narrow; he has no idea what I'm talking about. I cut a glare to Armando.

"Did you not talk to him; damn it, Jaffa. We want you to step into a new role and utilize your talents. We need to find the Russians, and so far, none of our best men can find the heads of the family."

"Anything for you."

"Let's stop all the depressing talk, let's get white girl wasted tonight and fuck like bunnies," Boo says, and I shake my head.

"I'm with him," Genie says.

Armando stands and heads over to the bar, I crane my neck to see what he is doing. The manager nods, and Armando slaps down a wad of cash on the bar. The bartender disappears, and when he comes back, he throws a set of keys at Jaffa.

"Everyone get the fuck out of my bar now!" the bartender yells. Patrons get up and leave, some whine, and he just removes a gun from under the bar and waves it in the air. As Armando walks back toward us, he smirks at me and pours us all a shot of whiskey.

"Tonight, we drink and fuck, and tomorrow, we go to war. Salute."

"Salute," we all chant in unison before throwing back our shots of whiskey. Boo starts stripping out of his clothes, and we all laugh at his usual antics to get into everyone's pants. He wastes no time at all when it comes to sex, and I don't blame him because the sex is fucking fantastic.

I never in my wildest dreams thought that I would be here, head of the mafia, starting a war with the Russians, dating four men, and happier than I have ever been in my life.

Jaye Stalker Links

Bookbub

Newsletter

Facebook

TikTok

Reader Group

Instagram

Merch Store

(All of my papcrbacks are for sale on my Merch store. These all come with my signature. Postage world wide.)

For spoilers and Trigger warnings for all of my series visit my website.
Website: www.jayeprattauthor.com

Melinda Stalker Links

Amazon
amazon.com/author/melindaterranova
Stalk me on Insta www.instagram.com/melinda.terrano-va.author
facebook: www.facebook.com/melindaterranovaauthor

Mel's Booknerds
https://www.facebook.com/groups/379989669242705/

OTHER BOOKS BY JAYE

<u>Standalones</u>

Sweetest Venom

Chad and his not harem

Street Rat

<u>Knox Academy</u>

<u>(Complete Series)</u>

F*ck You

F*ck Off

F*ck Yeah

F*ck Her

<u>Gifted, Obedient, Deadly, Students,</u>

(Complete Series)

G.O.D.S

Checkmate

Endgame

<u>Grand Ridge University</u>

Tens - The Invitation

Tens - The Takeover

With you I am home

(Complete Duet)

Boys like you

Girl Like me

Duet (recommended to read this version it has a bonus scene.)

OTHER BOOKS BY MELINDA

Savage Kings of St. Ivy

Corrupt Temptation - mybook.to/corrupttemptation

Savage - mybook.to/savagelies

Tainted - mybook.to/taintedpromises

Hateful Vengeance - https://amzn.to/3xVS35t

JAYE ACKNOWLEDGEMENTS

ACKNOWLEDGEMENTS

(Jaye Pratt)

My husband, I love you.

My children, for spending all of my money and making me work harder to be able to buy myself nice things.

Melinda, for agreeing to write this story with me and helping bring it to life. Boo is forever yours.

To my best friend Amber, for taking my calls and listening to mc bitch about being tired and wanting to give up.

My alpha readers, Patricia, Cheria, Rachel, Lena, Istha, Kristin without you ladies I would be lost. You always jump straight in and get shit done and I will be forever grateful.

My ARC readers, reviews are one of the most important parts of being an author and each and every one of you leaving reviews means so much more than you could ever know.

And last but not least my readers, for giving my stories a chance and investing your time into loving my characters as much as I do. If it wasn't for you I wouldn't have a career doing something that I love.

ABOUT THE AUTHORS

Jaye Pratt

Jaye is an Australian author who lives in Queensland. Her love of reading came later in life after her sister forced her to read the twilight saga and she hasn't looked back since. Reading has become an escape from reality, a way to relax and forget about life for a short while.

Jaye is a mother of six children and one grandchild, and she loves having a large family. If Jaye isn't writing you will find her being a referee to a handful of her children or being a mum taxi, dropping children at work or sport.

Melinda Terranova

Melinda is an author of Dark Romance & Mafia books with touch her and you die vibes. She resides on the sunny Gold Coast with her family & 3 fur babies. When she's not writing you can find her drinking coffee, eating cake & dreaming of her next holiday.

Made in the USA
Las Vegas, NV
29 January 2025

17195423R00127